WHEN CHOCOLATE IS NOT ENOUGH...

BY

NINA HARRINGTON

MILLS & BOON

All the characters in this book have no existence
outside the imagination of the author, and have
no relation whatsoever to anyone bearing the same
name or names. They are not even distantly inspired
by any individual known or unknown to the author,
and all the incidents are pure invention.

First published in Great Britain 2012
by Mills & Boon, an imprint of Harlequin (UK) Limited.
Large Print edition 2012
Harlequin (UK) Limited, Eton House,
18-24 Paradise Road, Richmond, Surrey TW9 1SR

© Nina Harrington 2012

ISBN: 978 0 263 22597 6

Harlequin (UK) policy is to use papers that are natural,
renewable and recyclable products and made from
wood grown in sustainable forests. The logging and
manufacturing process conform to the legal environmental
regulations of the country of origin.

Printed and bound in Great Britain
by CPI Antony Rowe, Chippenham, Wiltshire

CHAPTER ONE

MAKE your hen party extra special with our Luxury Chocolate Man Parts!

Max Treveleyn stopped in his tracks and stared in astonishment at the espresso and cream-coloured banner splashed across the top of the food stall promoting 'Tara's Tantalising Party Treats'.

This was central London, and party catering was big business. But 'man parts'? It was the last thing he had expected to see at a classy organic food festival.

Max peered over the heads of the ladies who were clustered around the stall, jostling for a position in line to try the samples before making their selections. He didn't want to think about what they would do with them when they got home—but this stall was certainly doing brisk business for a Monday lunchtime.

He glanced swiftly at the digital clock on the

wall above the entrance to the underground station. He had twenty minutes at most to find the art gallery where he had arranged to meet his ex-wife Kate for lunch—but he could spare a few of those minutes to find out just how far organic chocolate had come since his last visit to London.

It was only as he got closer that Max realised that a short, bubbly blonde girl was running the stall, completely concealed behind the crush of customers who were waving cash and pointing furiously at the trays of remarkably life-size and anatomically correct shapes.

The blonde was wearing a T-shirt with the words 'Tara's Treats' across the front. In another place, with a different audience, those words might be misconstrued—especially since the T-shirt was rather on the small side for a girl with a substantial bosom.

Perhaps this was the famous Tara herself?

The party treats seemed to be going down extremely well, and it took Max a few minutes to shuffle forward and find a gap in the queue. If only the organic chocolate *he* made was as popular as this he would never have to worry again about the future of his cocoa plantation back in St Lucia. But, then again, perhaps moulded chocolate man parts were not exactly the premium outlet he needed to bring in extra income.

The blonde looked up at him, blinked twice, then grinned. 'Hello, handsome. Looking for something for your stag party? I have just the thing.' She reached over the counter and pulled out a tray of milk chocolate shapes which literally took Max's breath away. 'It's your lucky day—we have a special offer on all body parts. How many would you like?'

He coughed politely before shaking his head. 'Um… Thank you, but I don't need any milk chocolate toes today—although I am sure they are quite delicious,' he said, when he finally managed to get some air into his lungs. 'But would you mind if I took some photographs of your stall? It certainly is…er…different.'

She glared at him open-mouthed for a second, before throwing her head back and laughing out loud with a laugh that echoed around the London street where the festival was being held. It was the kind of laugh that meant that she had to snort in a breath halfway through.

'Daisy! One of our gentleman browsers wants to photograph your chocs. Are you okay with that?'

Max looked over the blonde's shoulder towards a tall brunette wearing chef's trousers and a white jacket, who was rummaging around inside large plastic food boxes. As the brunette flicked a glance towards Max her eyes smiled at the same time as her mouth, crinkling the sides of her cheeks into a rosy glow, so that when she spoke her face was animated and full of laughter and fun.

'Only if he buys something. Here.' She whisked around and presented him with a box of flesh-coloured chocolate half domes made into bosoms, with a circle of caramel icing in the centre. A dark chocolate cocoa bean added the final realistic touch. 'I also have them in a mocha choc blend, if you would prefer that,' she added. 'Or perhaps the lovely Tara can tempt you with some of each? All organic chocolate, of course, and hand-made by the person you are looking at.'

The brunette waved the box under Max's nose, and without intending to he half closed his eyes and inhaled the wonderful aroma of fine chocolate and soft fruit. His nose came a lot closer than he had planned to one of the chocolate cocoa beans, and he physically recoiled the instant he opened his eyes and focused on what was in front of him.

'Wow. That chocolate smells amazing. And is that a touch of raspberry?' he asked.

'Fresh organic raspberry coulis and vanilla extract.' She nodded. 'But tell me now if you want some, because all my boobs are selling out fast ahead of the stag and hen party season. June is such a wonderful month to get married, don't you think?'

A visual flash of memory hit Max hard. Sparkling champagne, kilts and plaid, and Scottish dancing in the tiny frigid village hall chosen by Kate's parents for their wedding. Their June wedding had turned out to be cold, wet and windy, but he had not felt it for a moment. They had both been so young and idealistic, with crazy dreams of their new life in St Lucia.

Shame that the hard reality of that life had burst their bubble only too quickly.

A bustle of ladies looking for unique party treats jostled him gently, and as he turned to acknowledge their apologies he realised that the brunette was still waiting for him to give her an answer.

'Hello? Are you still with me?' she asked with a smile. 'You seemed to be in a world of your own for a moment there.'

'You reminded me about my own wedding. And you were quite right. June can be a great month to get married.' He swallowed down a moment of angst, then looked up at her with a twisted grin and a wink. 'Thank you for that.'

'All part of the service. And...er...' she gestured with her head towards the tray of chocolate shapes '...how many would you like? A pair is usual, three is a bit kinky, and four would be greedy. But, hey, go for it.'

He looked up at her—and then really looked. She had stepped into the sunshine, and now he could see that her hair was not brown but a deep russet-red colour, and just long enough to flick out at the neck of her heart-shaped face. A pair of wide green eyes smiled back at him, and under his gaze her mouth lifted to create a triangle of creases from her small chin to her rosy cheeks. Somehow he felt able to put aside that lingering sense of failure and regret at the breakdown of his marriage and enjoy the moment.

'I'm sure your—your boobs are very nice,' Max stuttered, creating a titter from the other customers. 'I mean the chocolate boobs, of course. But I only enjoy organic dark chocolate. The darker the better.'

Her face dropped, and he instantly felt guilty about wasting her time when he truly did not want to buy anything. 'Although there is something you might be able to help me with.'

'Really?' she asked, her eyebrows high. 'I find that hard to believe, considering that not even my special boobs can tempt you.'

When she smiled one side of her mouth lifted higher than the other, and he noticed that the end of her fair-skinned nose was peeling a little, with a scattering of freckles.

Red hair, green eyes and freckles.

Oh, no. *Killer.*

His heart started beating just a little faster—but enough for him to look away and pretend to glance over the banners on the stall. He was obviously a lot more tired than he'd thought he was if a young woman's smile could turn on the switches he had firmly locked into the closed position.

No more girlfriends. He had already sacrificed one marriage to his obsession with growing cocoa and had no intention of going there again.

He quickly coughed, to cover up his embarrassment, before answering her question. 'Do you have something for a children's birthday party? My daughter will be eight next week.'

'Ah, a family man,' she replied in a softer voice, and her shoulders relaxed. 'Why didn't you say so? We sold out of most of our children's treats earlier this morning, but let me just check to see if we have any animal shapes left.' She dived back into the plastic boxes, probably not aware that her chef's trousers stretched a little too tightly over a very pert rear end as she bent over.

'Teddy bears or bunny rabbits?' she replied in a singsong voice as she rummaged. 'White or milk chocolate? Oh—and a few very special dark chocolate-dipped raisins. Except we call them rabbit droppings. Kids love that.' She grinned. 'I would recommend the rabbits.'

Pulling out a flat tray, she stepped towards Max and he peered inside. Beautifully formed milk chocolate bite-size rabbits with pink-tinted white chocolate ears stared back at him.

'Those look terrific,' he said. 'I'll take them all—and a bag of the raisins. Do you mind if I try one? Denise…?'

'Be my guest—and it's Daisy, not Denise,' she answered, and presented him with a small tray of the chocolate raisins. 'Tara and I love catering for children's parties. They are so much fun.' Daisy winked. 'It would make a wonderful birthday present. That little girl will be the envy of all of her friends.'

Max was just about to open his mouth to tell her that he owned a cocoa plantation in St Lucia, so Freya's friends already thought that she had a mountain of chocolate bars stashed in her bedroom cupboard, when Daisy picked up a dark chocolate-covered raisin and without hesitating or asking for permission popped it into his mouth.

Her fingers slid against his lips, and for a fraction of a second Max felt a real connection which was so elemental and raw that he covered up his discomfort by focusing on the food.

Organic chocolate. It had a lot to answer for. But it had been so long...

'What do you think?' she asked, completely unaware that she was responsible for the hot discomfort inside his chest. 'For adult parties I soak the fruit in alcohol, to offset the sweetness, but this rabbit poo is apple juice flavour. It seems to work.'

Max chewed the raisin for a few seconds, then swallowed. 'Wow!' He blinked and tried to hide a grimace. 'I have to admit I'm more used to bitter chocolate, so that amount of sugar comes as a shock. And I'm trying to persuade my daughter not to eat so many sweet foods, so you will excuse me if I only take a few of the raisins.'

'I beg your pardon?'

He shook his head. 'I don't want to be responsible for a troop of eight-year-olds high on sugar and additives.'

There was a hiss from Tara as she whizzed past with an empty tray.

'Whoops. Dangerous ground. You just said the A word. Be prepared to duck.'

Max turned back to Daisy, who was breathing rather heavily, her head on one side, eyes narrowed. Her voice had a definite frosty tone to it when she replied. 'First of all, the only additives I use in my chocolate are organic fruits and sugars. And secondly all raisins are sweet. That's their job. And children adore them. I tried using plain chocolate on its own and they were left on the plate every time.'

'That's a pity,' he replied, and lifted up another covered raisin and held it under his nose. 'I can't even smell subtle flavours in the chocolate. Perhaps you could try a less bitter cocoa bean? That way you could cut down on the sugar but still have the cocoa flavour. A single estate variety would work really well.'

The brunette's mouth dropped open for a second, before she lifted her chin and crossed her arms.

'Oh, really? Do go on,' Daisy replied in a *faux*-sweet voice. 'I'm quite fascinated to hear how I can improve the recipe for a chocolate coating I have just spent the last six months working on. I can hardly *wait* to hear what other little gems of advice you might have for me.'

Max cleared his throat. He had said the wrong thing again—but he liked a challenge. Time to throw the ball back and see how high it bounced. 'I'm just saying that it might not be the best choice for coating dried fruit. And this *is* a fine-quality organic chocolate, isn't it?'

Daisy did not have to answer, because at that moment Tara laughed out loud as she served a young man in a slick business suit with four of the boobs Max had just been sniffing. 'It certainly is,' she said. 'And it costs me an absolute fortune every week. But Daisy insists that our Belgian chocolate has to be the best. Your money won't be wasted.' Tara pointed at Daisy with her tongs. 'And you, young lady, have an appointment somewhere else. Go—scoot. I'll take care of your gentleman friend here. And thanks again for helping me out.'

Daisy glanced at her watch and gasped. 'If that's the real time, I am toast.' She popped an extra raisin into the tray of rabbits and pushed it towards Max. 'I hope that your daughter has a lovely birthday party. Even with all of that sweet mystery chocolate which is sure to rot her teeth. Bye.' And with one swift movement she untied her apron, waved to him with the hand that was not occupied in swooping up her bag, and was out through the back of the stall before Max could reply.

He had barely regained his senses when he looked around to find the blonde standing in front of him, with her tongs raised in one gloved hand like a surgeon preparing to operate.

'Hello again. My name's Tara. What other tantalising treats can I tempt you with today?'

Max sauntered down the sunlit London pavement, swinging his Tara's Treats carrier bag in one hand and his luggage over one shoulder. He was going to be late for his lunch date with Kate, but it had been worth it to meet the lovely Daisy and Tara.

Things had certainly changed in the artisan chocolate world if those two ladies were typical examples. Most of the chocolatiers he knew were professional older men, running chains of chocolate shops, or buyers from large-scale manufacturers of famous brands of chocolate being sold around the world in their millions. Not a moulded bosom in sight. More was the pity. But those girls had the right idea. Chocolate was a pleasure to be enjoyed—it should be fun! He was going to enjoy sharing these rabbits with Kate and Freya.

Max caught his reflection in the plate glass window of a designer clothing shop and winced. He ran a rough hand across his chin. Not his best look. He had barely slept these last few days, bringing in the cocoa harvest and collapsing into bed out of physical exhaustion only when it became too dark to work safely.

Perhaps he should have taken the time to wash and shave at the airport after his red eye flight before catching the tube into London? Kate might forgive him for not having the kind of haircut and dress sense of her new boyfriend, who was a big City banker, but she would mind if he turned up at a smart art gallery and restaurant looking scruffy and dishevelled. He owed her a lot more than that. Especially when she had specifically asked him if they could talk over lunch before he picked their daughter up from school.

A broad grin flashed across Max's face, wiping away his feelings of anxiety and concern.

He might have been an idiot in some ways, but he had done something amazing when he'd married Kate and they'd brought a ray of sunshine like Freya Treveleyn into the world. Almost eight years old, bright as a button, and so very, very precious. Some mornings, when it was lashing down with tropical rain, the cocoa beans were going rotten and he was struggling to pay his workers' wages, just the sight of that little girl's photograph on his bedside table was enough to get him back to work.

Freya was why he fought and fought to make his organic cocoa plantation a success. She was his inspiration, his motivation, and the reason he stuck it out. Even if it meant that he had to leave her with her mother in London for most of the year.

A cluster of tourists blocked his way and Max dodged onto the road for a few seconds, watching out for the madcap cyclists, London buses and black cabs as he did so.

He had never been comfortable in this fabulous city, with its never-ending stream of action and life, the noise and bustle of people and traffic. His home was the Caribbean forest plantation house where he had grown up. The only real noise pollution there came from the flocks of wild brightly coloured parrots which descended on the treetops to squawk at the workers when they disturbed their calm life. Now he tried to block out the cacophony of noise from the traffic and the crush of people which seemed to deafen him, and was grateful when he spotted the entrance to the central London art gallery.

Minutes later Max hoisted his bag higher onto his shoulder and looked around the crowded restaurant until he spotted the woman he had once called his wife, perched on the edge of a dining chair at the best table in the restaurant.

Catherine Ormandy Treveleyn was wearing a caramel-coloured linen shift dress, gold sandals and gold jewellery. Her long straight blonde hair fell in a waterfall over her shoulders. She was elegant. Sophisticated.

But to him she would always be the backpacking university student who had sauntered onto the plantation on her way to meet up with her friends on the beach. She had lost her way. And he had lost his head and his heart the same day.

This was the woman who'd had dreams of running an eco-cocoa plantation in the West Indies under the Caribbean sun.

Until it had all gone wrong.

Until she had decided that her future was in London, and that he could either come with her or stay in St Lucia with his one true love. The plantation. She'd used to call it the mistress she could not compete against—and she was right. He had sacrificed his family for that estate.

All the more reason for him to make sure that the estate did not fail.

Kate looked up from her glass of wine just as he stepped forward. She glanced at her watch with a smile and a gentle shake of her head as he bent to kiss her cheek.

'Sorry to keep you waiting, gorgeous.' Max smiled. 'You are looking as lovely as ever. My feeble excuse is the organic food festival in the street outside the tube station. Can you forgive me? I picked up something for Freya on the way.'

Kate kissed him warmly on the cheek. 'Time-keeping has never been your strength. I can see that you're still not wearing that watch I gave you for Christmas.'

Max shrugged. 'Watches and clocks are for other people. You should know that.' He gave her a sly wink as he sat down. 'How is our little girl today?'

Her reply was a gentle nod of the head and a wide grin. 'She's on fine form. And very much looking forward to seeing you. Do you still plan to pick her up from school?'

She passed him the bread basket and he inhaled the delicious aroma of freshly baked rosemary focaccia with a sigh. He nodded absentmindedly and peered at the food on the table, suddenly famished. 'Absolutely. This looks good.'

'The food here is terrific, and I took the liberty of ordering your favourite lasagne *al forno*. One of the few treats that's hard to find on your tropical paradise.'

'You know me too well,' Max replied, and

passed her the paper bag that Tara had given him. 'In that case I trade one lasagne for a bag of chocolate rabbits. Can I add these to the birthday feast next week? I know that you can buy organic chocolates anywhere in London these days, but the stall was run by two pretty girls and the bunnies look almost good enough for our daughter to eat.'

Kate peered into the bag, then stared at him across the table. 'You? Buying chocolate? Well, this is new. The very thought of a supermarket chocolate bar sends you into a tizzy. They must be good—either that or the girls were particularly pretty. And please don't growl at me like that.' She reached out and lifted a curl of hair from his collar. 'Even with hair that long, some girl might give you a second look.'

Max snorted a dismissive reply. 'One special lady is more than enough in my life right now. Do you remember that special birthday present she wanted?'

When his ex-wife raised a querying eyebrow, Max patted his rucksack on the floor. 'I finished carving a pair of jungle parrots last week. They are just like the ones she liked in the photo I sent her. I hope she likes them.'

'Of course she will. But don't be too disappointed if she prefers the new games console that Anton has bought her. She's nearly eight years old, Max. Her life revolves around computer games, schoolwork and her friends. St Lucia is just a place on the map where her dad goes for weeks or months at a time. I'm sorry if that sounds hard, but I don't want you to think that she is ungrateful,' Kate said gently.

'Even more reason why I should take Freya to spend the summer holidays with me on the island. She's old enough now to watch out for danger, and the other kids on the farm would show her how much fun it can be.'

Kate sat back and sipped her chilled white wine. 'We've been through this before, Max. July and August are your peak harvest times. I know that you'll do everything you can to keep Freya safe, but you would be too busy to be with her every second of the day, and the island is a dangerous place for a city child.'

'You're right,' Max replied, his arms stretched out across the table. 'We do cut the cocoa during the summer. But nothing is more important to me than our little girl. And if I do get called out, the ladies on the plantation have been begging me to bring Freya to visit. I could have a swat team of expert grandmothers on standby, ready and willing to step in at a moment's notice. Serious cossetting and overfeeding would be involved. She'd be totally spoiled!'

'Well,' Kate acknowledged, 'that is one option. But, speaking of the summer holidays, I did ask you here so that we could talk without Freya in the room, because there is something I need to share with you.'

She paused, and Max noticed that a vein in her temple was throbbing in tune with the rate of her breathing. A clear sign that she was anxious about what she was about to say. *Interesting.*

'Come on, Kate. What do you want to tell me? Get it over with.'

Her shoulders seemed to relax for a few seconds, and she made eye contact before speaking again. 'Anton has asked me to marry him, and I have said yes. We're choosing the ring next week, and I would like to tell Freya on her birthday as a sort of a surprise present. But I wanted you to be the first to know.'

Married!

It was as though someone had tipped an ice bucket of chilled water over his head.

He had always known that this was possible. They were both single now, and she was a lovely woman who enjoyed her social circle in London. But dating a French banker was a lot different from becoming engaged to one.

He was happy for her—happy that she had found someone who loved her and she could love in return—but he had not expected to have to face the reality of that possibility so soon.

It was as though the thin line which still connected them as friends who had become lovers, then friends again, suddenly seemed to stretch thinner and thinner, until it was almost at breaking point.

They had worked hard and talked through the night so many times to keep their friendship alive for the sake of their daughter. Suddenly it felt as though he was losing control.

And there was not one thing that he could do to change it.

She was looking at him now, her upper teeth taking the edge from her perfect lipstick. Expecting some response. He had to say something. Anything.

The air between them positively crackled with tension.

Flicking back his hair, Max dropped his head and laughed out loud.

'Married? No! Wow—that's wonderful. Congratulations, Kate. I am happy for you. Anton is a very lucky man. Can I be your manly maid of honour?'

Until that moment he had not even noticed that Kate had been holding her breath, but her gentle giggle told him everything that he needed to know. She had been nervous about telling him. Nervous that she might upset him. Knowing that it *would* upset him—which was so crazy that it made his head spin. Their marriage had broken up because of his obsession— his failure, his neglect. She deserved a chance at happiness.

'No. You cannot be my maid of honour, but thank you for your understanding, Max. This is an awkward situation, isn't it? It's only been three years since we split up, and here I am getting married again.'

Instantly he stretched out his hand and gave her fingers a quick squeeze, before drawing back and replying with a smile. 'It's okay, Kate. Really. I'm genuinely happy for you. The last few years have been tough on you, and I haven't been around much to help. You deserve to be happy. Anton seems like a steady bloke, and he would be an idiot not to be crazy about you. Good luck to you both.'

He raised his water glass in a toast, just for something to do with his hands, while his head caught up with the implications.

'So when is the wedding? Are you planning a spectacular event or something small and cosy?'

'A huge extravaganza, of course! Anton's family have offered us the use of their château in Provence, and are paying for everything as their wedding gift. You should see the house, Max—it is totally stunning and the perfect setting for a wedding. It's really going to be magical.'

'A château?' He coughed and spluttered.

'Well, that will be quite a change from your first wedding. That old hall was freezing.'

'I know!' She laughed, then ran a hand through her hair nervously. 'As for the timing…? That is my next piece of news. I know I'm about to suggest something which will probably upset you, because—well, we are planning to have the wedding next spring, and I would like Freya to spend the whole summer with us at the château in France this year.'

Max put down his glass and took a breath, counted to five before answering. 'I thought we agreed at Christmas that Freya would spend all of the summer holidays with me at the cottage, since you refuse to let me take her to the island? That way you can have some personal time with Anton.'

'Yes, we did. But that's all changed now, Max. Anton's family only meet once a year at the château, to spend the summer together, and I know they can't wait to meet her.'

Kate was beaming across at him with such delight that the warmth in her voice went some way to melting the ice that had started to form around his heart.

'You need not worry about her being on her own at the château. Anton has lots of young nieces and nephews for her to play with, and she will be totally spoiled. This is the first chance she will have to meet all of Anton's family. Her new family. She'll love it,' Kate said.

Max sighed out loud and fought to keep a caustic mixture of anger, loss and disappointment out of his voice. 'Well, that ties it. How could she possibly choose between a French château, being spoilt rotten with a whole new family, and roughing it in my nana's ramshackle old cottage in the middle of nowhere, with only her old dad to entertain her? The fact that I have been planning this holiday since Christmas doesn't really feature, does it? Even if it means that I won't have any time with her before she goes back to school in September.'

Kate looked sympathetic but determined. 'I know this is hard on you, but having Freya with us this summer will make her feel part of the plans for the wedding. Part of the changes in our life, I suppose.'

Max tapped his fingertips on the table before giving in with good grace. 'I don't like this,

Kate, but I suppose it isn't about what I want any longer, but what is best for Freya. And then what happens? Are you planning to stay in the London house after you marry?'

She nodded. 'Anton has a great job here in the City. There's plenty of room, and Freya wouldn't be moving away from her school and her friends. I think that this is going to work, Max. I really do.'

Max rearranged the cutlery on the table as he formed his next question, his eyes focused on the perfect alignment of the knife and fork set. 'I trust your judgement, Katie—I always have. I know that you wouldn't make Anton part of Freya's life unless you were sure that he was going to be a positive influence. But what about me? Where do I fit in?'

A lump formed in his throat as he asked the question he most dreaded hearing the answer to.

'How soon do you think it will be before my daughter starts calling Anton Dad?'

Kate grasped his fingers, forcing him to lift his head, then lowered her face and looked up into his eyes.

'Anton knows that you are part of our lives.

He is very fond of Freya—yes, she will be sharing her home with him, and seeing him every day, but she knows who her father is. I'll make sure that she never gets confused about that.'

He nodded, not trusting his own voice at that moment. 'Thanks, but I think that we should both be there when you tell Freya about the wedding. Help her to understand that I am not going to walk out on her, or pass her over to Anton like some unwanted gift. I am still her dad and I will always love her. That doesn't go away.'

He'd tried to keep the pain out of his voice, but Kate looked at him in concern. 'She knows that. We raised a very clever little girl. This is about what is best for our daughter. But shall we talk about that later? Let's enjoy our meal. I hear that they have a wonderful new chocolate chef...'

The stunning aroma of bubbling grilled cheese and meaty pasta sauce saved his day as the waiter presented their food, blocking his view of the woman who had paid the price for his obsession with a cocoa farm.

The woman who was about to present their daughter with a new live-in stepfather.

She smiled at him across the table. 'Now. Tell me all about this conference on organic cocoa that you are whizzing off to at the end of the week. Cornwall, isn't it? It sounds so exciting. I want to know everything!'

CHAPTER TWO

DAISY FLYNN squeezed into the cramped office at the side of the restaurant kitchen and collapsed down on a tiny metal stool. She had made it with only minutes to spare, after a mad dash back to her kitchen to pick up an emergency supply of chocolate desserts for the restaurant. The head chef at the restaurant in one of London's premier art galleries had become one of her best customers, so this was one delivery that she was happy to make in person.

Marco had given her the chance to produce a range of artisan chocolates and desserts that she had only dreamt of in her father's bakery all those years ago. And every one of them was perfect practice for the only thing she had truly ever wanted. The one thing she had slaved and practised and experimented for day after day, week after week, month after month. Year after year—and it *had* been years since Paris.

Her very own chocolate shop, serving droolicious artisan chocolates made from the finest organic chocolate to her secret and unique recipes and designs. Her shop was going to be every girl's fantasy of chocolate heaven.

That was her dream. And she was almost there!

She had the recipes. She had ideas for the shop and what its tantalising interior would look like. She could even imagine what it would smell like, with all the chocolates on display.

It would be amazing.

All she needed now was a great reliable source of organic fine cocoa and she would be ready to walk into the bank with a business plan that would knock their socks off. Plus a few samples of the actual goods if the discussions got tricky.

It was going to happen—because she was going to *make* it happen.

She would finally be able to show the world what a baker's daughter from a small country town could do, given the chance—just as her dad had predicted she would. On her own. She didn't need some famous-name chocolatier taking the credit—not again.

It was so sad that her father hadn't lived long enough to see her achieve her dream. Even if it did mean that today she'd had to jog most of the way through the streets of London with her precious cargo of desserts. She was tired, hot, out of breath and moist in places she would rather not be moist—but close enough to her goal to put a smile on her face.

In fact Daisy was still catching her breath when Marco waltzed in, wiping his hands on the towel tucked into the waistband of his apron and then reaching across the desk to shake Daisy's hand.

'Thanks for coming at such short notice, Daisy. It has been mad out there today, and we are fully booked with coach parties of tourists every lunch and dinner service for the next two weeks.' Marco raised his right hand. 'I'm not complaining. Far from it. But it leaves me with a problem. A big one.' And he pointed straight at Daisy. 'Namely you, young lady.'

Daisy swallowed down her anxiety, but leant forward to reply. 'Me? Is there a problem with your order? I checked it through with the sous chef when I delivered the dessert trays. I'm sorry if...'

Marco waved his fingers at her and sat back in his chair. 'No, no. There is no problem with your food at all. In fact it is just the opposite. I knew when I tasted your work that the chocolate dessert range would be popular with the ladies who lunch, but I had no clue just how many portions we would serve. You've seen the orders double these past few weeks, and we actually ran out of that flourless melting middle cake last night. Our guests were not happy. And that brings me to why I've asked you to hang around for a few minutes.'

He leant his elbows on top of a pile of papers on the desk and formed a tent with his clever long fingers. 'I have a proposition for you. Right now I order your chocolate from Tara's company, and that was okay for the occasional one off event. But that was before I found out just how good you really were. We look after four art galleries in this city, and the bottom line is we need a professional chocolatier like yourself heading up our patisserie section.'

The breath froze in Daisy's lungs as she tried

to come up with a suitable reply, but she was too stunned to do more than stare.

'Oh, I know,' Marco said, flicking away her silent protestations. 'You want to open a chocolate shop with your name over the door. You made that clear the first day you walked into my kitchen—and there is nothing wrong with that. Call it Flynn's Fancies, or whatever. But think about *this.*'

His long arms pressed hard against the papers on the desk and Marco's intense dark brown eyes seemed to burn a hole in Daisy's forehead.

'What if we put your name on the menu and make this a full-time job, with your own kitchen area and a sous chef to help you? You could reach hundreds of diners every day *and* have the flexibility to experiment with new ideas. Buy the chocolate you want. Best of ingredients. Best of everything. The job is yours if you want it.' Then he gave a short shrug and grinned. 'You can breathe again now.'

Daisy realised that she had been holding her breath the whole time the head chef had been talking, and grasped hold of the desk as she sucked in enough air to help clear her dizzy head.

'Wow. Thank you. I certainly wasn't expecting an offer like this. I am flattered—I really am—but as I said before my heart is still set on opening my own artisan chocolate shop. The restaurant work is brilliant, and we really are grateful for it, but if I did come here it would only be for a short time, and Tara would lose the business after I left. I'm not sure that it's fair to either of us. Does that make sense?'

Marco sniffed once before replying, 'How close are you to opening your own shop?'

Daisy pushed her hands flat under her bottom to stop herself from bouncing with excitement. 'So close I can feel it. The real problem is that I want to make my own chocolate. I mean—from scratch. Right now I am buying commercial blends and they are good—very good—but they're not *there* yet. It could take years to achieve that perfect blend. Or it could be months. I simply don't know.'

Marco's reply was to fling open his arms wide as he rocked back in his chair. 'Then come and work for us. We can buy in bulk, get good deals from specialist suppliers, and I can guarantee you some room to experiment.' He waved his right hand in the air with a casual twist. 'Think of our diners as your product testers. We win—you win. And we can still use Tara for other things. It could work very well.'

He paused and pursed his lips before shrugging.

'It makes sense for us to find a wonderful dessert chef to look after all of our catering operations, and I would like it to be you. But if you decide not to take up my offer there is a long list of other chefs who would like to show us what they can do—and some of them have worked with chocolate before. They could come up with some interesting recipes.'

'But not the same as mine.' Daisy smiled, her ego marginally more inflated than normal.

'Perhaps not. But still fantastic. And then, of course, we would not need to use outside supplies. Perhaps you should talk this over with Tara? She might have an opinion about that.'

'Oh. Yes. Tara. Of course.' Daisy's heart sank. 'How long…? When do you need to hear back from me?'

'I was hoping you would call me in the next few weeks.' Marco smiled persuasively. 'It can be fun working here. We have great customers who love their food. Let me help you to make up your mind. We only have a few lunch guests left, but some have ordered your chocolate and almond cake. How would you like to go out into the restaurant and hear what they have to say about your work? You might find that interesting.'

Daisy blinked, and swallowed down a lump of panic before squeaking out, 'Do you mean right now? I'm not sure I'm ready for that.'

Except Marco had already made the decision, and was on his feet rooting though a pile of chef's jackets hanging up behind the office door. 'This is your chance to hear what the customers think about your work face to face. Here you go. This one should fit nicely. Ready?'

Before Daisy could change her mind she'd exchanged jackets and followed one of London's most highly respected chefs out into the kitchen. Peering out over the serving hatch, she could see a few tables were still occupied.

Marco wiggled his fingers towards a table on

the left. 'Go and have a chat. You never know—the restaurant trade might be perfect for you after all.'

'That table?' Daisy stepped forward nervously and peered across the room towards a charming young couple who were obviously having a long, romantic lunch together.

The man's back was to her, but the woman was dressed so elegantly that Daisy automatically ran her hands down the front of her clothing and checked that her uniform was clean and tidy. She knew the sort. This girl looked as though she had been born with perfect poise and style and did not have to try very hard to be stunning in any situation. In other words exactly the sort of girl who, quite innocently, always made her feel totally clumsy, tongue-tied and inadequate—like a country bumpkin out for a spree in the city, who did not truly belong there.

Then the man turned slightly and she took a closer look. There was no mistaking the shaggy, long dark blond hair, and the heavy stubble that spread above those bow lips, across a square chin and almost to the end of his prominent cheekbones.

It was the man from the food stall who had bought the chocolate rabbits. His black jacket was hanging over the back of his chair, and he was wearing a fitted black cotton long-sleeved shirt which had seen better and cleaner days. On any other man it would have looked scruffy and washed out, and hardly suitable for a lovely restaurant lunch. But drat if it did not suit his broad shoulders as he stretched forward. How irritating was that?

His hair looked as though he had just woken up and raked it through with his fingers, but for some reason the tousled look fitted him perfectly.

She gulped down something close to apprehension. Um. She had a fair idea of exactly what *his* response would be if she marched up and asked him what he thought about the chocolate dessert.

'Forget that couple,' the chef whispered in her ear, and Daisy breathed out a sigh of relief. 'They are still waiting for dessert service. But those two ladies over there are just paying the bill. Perfect. Try them first, before looping back. Have fun!'

Max had gone through a huge portion of lasagne, two servings of delicious warm bread, and had just inhaled a platter of cheese and biscuits when the waiter placed a dark circle of aromatic dense chocolate loveliness in front of Kate, then stepped around with his portion.

Max could already smell the chocolate, and instantly pushed his cheese plate to one side, ready for his dessert.

Kate responded with a small laugh. 'I know that you are dying to tell me everything about this chocolate, so I'm going to simply sit here and drink my coffee while you enjoy yourself. Feel free to dig in any time you like. You *do* know that I shall insist that the chefs use Treveleyn Estate chocolate for my wedding reception, don't you?'

Max chuckled. 'Of course. You can consider it my wedding present to you both. So, what do we have here?'

He lifted the plate so that he could inhale the fragrance of the chocolate base, trying to ignore the sideways glances from the waiting staff and other diners, then cut straight across the middle of the circular cake, separated the two halves and tried smelling it again.

Oh, wow, that was good. *Seriously good.* A chocolate and almond liqueur was laced through the mixture, but it was not too powerful to conceal the wonderful spicy and deep aroma of the chocolate.

Only then did he scoop up a generous bite-sized portion and wrap his mouth around the cake, before sliding the spoon away to leave… a small miracle. The smooth, smooth chocolate melted on his tongue, releasing more and more layers of flavour. Not too sweet, and certainly not sickly, the cocoa butter had been blended with cream, finely ground nuts and butter to create the closest thing to a praline chocolate centre he had ever eaten. It was superb.

The chef who had made this knew how to blend cocoa beans from different varieties to create a perfectly aromatic but smooth flavour—intense but enjoyable. Stunning.

Max immediately took a larger spoonful, then another, and savoured every morsel before looking up at his bemused former wife, who had barely taken a single spoonful.

'Now, *that* was seriously good.'

'Thought you'd like it. But I have to watch my weight—so, please, finish off mine as well. You know you want to.'

'Pass it over! This is superb. In fact,' he mumbled through tiny scrapings of cake, trying to make it last and prolong the pleasure, 'this is so good it has given me an idea for the conference at the weekend. Kate, would you mind if I left you to your coffee for ten minutes? I need to track down the dessert chef who made this.'

'Well, now's your chance.' Kate nodded over his shoulder. 'She's on her way over to speak to us.'

Max whipped around in his chair, and was halfway to a standing position when he lifted his chin and found himself staring at the white-coated chest of a girl he recognised only too well from the organic chocolate stall. She was wearing the gallery's restaurant jacket now, but there was no mistaking that hair and those stunning eyes.

'Daisy? What are you doing here?'

The startled look on her face as she took a step backwards was not perhaps the best reaction he could have hoped for, but it did give him a few seconds to connect his mouth and his brain.

'Sorry, you startled me. I had no idea that you worked here as well.' He tried to recover with a grin.

'Just visiting,' Daisy replied, and scooted around to the other side of the table to shake Kate's hand. 'Good afternoon. My name is Daisy Flynn, and I am the chocolatier for this restaurant. I notice that you ordered the chocolate and almond cake? I do hope that you enjoyed it.'

'Oh, it was absolutely delicious. Catherine Ormandy. Lovely to meet you. In fact I was just telling Max here that the restaurant has quite a reputation for its wonderful chocolate desserts. Do you make them all yourself? Because they really are very special.'

'You are very kind, Mrs Ormandy. My colleague Tara Hamilton and I run a company specialising in organic party food. But I do create all the chocolates and desserts by hand in our own kitchens. As well as party treats. In fact, I think your husband has already sampled some of my work—at our stall this morning.'

With that she stepped to one side and looked at him with a fixed, closed-mouth smile. 'He seemed to think that I was intent on poisoning the tastebuds of the younger generation with sugar and additives. Isn't that true, Mr Ormandy? I do hope that you're not feeling ill after scoffing my chocolate dessert. Shame that my creamy boobs were not to your taste.'

Without giving him a chance to reply, Daisy swivelled back to Kate. She smiled warmly at her slightly stunned expression, just as Marco came over and stood by their table.

'Ah. I see you have met our chocolate chef. Ms Flynn took top marks in the master chocolatier awards ceremony only last year, after training at Barone Fine Chocolate in Paris. We are hoping to persuade her to work with us a lot more.'

'Thank you, Chef,' Daisy said, and looked at the female diner while discreetly avoiding eye contact with her husband on the other side of the table. 'It was lovely to meet you, Mrs Ormandy.

I do hope that you have a splendid afternoon and will visit the restaurant again soon. Now, if you'll excuse me, I will leave you in Marco's capable hands.' And with that she turned and walked slowly and calmly, head high, back in the direction of the kitchens.

She had almost made it as far as the swing door leading to the kitchen when a loud male voice called out behind her in a very distinctive accent she had heard before.

'Miss Flynn? If you could wait a moment? Miss Flynn?'

Fighting against her sudden desire to reach for the nearest heavy frying pan in the kitchen, Daisy stopped and inhaled deeply.

This man was Marco's customer—and she owed Marco several favours. Not including the job offer. Insulting one of his diners was not perhaps the best way to win more orders from the restaurant chain. Even if this particular diner seemed to think that he knew more about chocolate than she did. At least his lovely wife had been charming. And he *had* bought some of her rabbits for his little girl, who probably idolised him.

That was it. He was a family man. Happily married. And one of Marco's paying customers.

Be nice to the people who pay your wages, Daisy.

So she fixed a professional, all-weather, no matter how great the provocation neutral smile on her lips, lifted her chin and turned slowly around so that she was not blocking the kitchen door.

And instantly had to fling her back flat against the wall to stop him from sending her flying.

He was caught out by her sudden stop and grabbed hold of both her arms to stop himself falling and crushing them both on the floor. In the process he drew her to him so quickly that Daisy barely had time to breathe before she found herself pressed up against the front of his shirt.

Both of them sucked in a shocked breath, and for a moment time seemed to stand still before he took a step back to create an appropriate space between them.

Back at the food stall she had been too busy to notice more than his unruly long dark blond hair hanging from a side parting almost to the collar of his black shirt. But up close he seemed to tower over her, even in his fairly flat black boots. He had to be well over six feet tall, but it was the sheer breadth of the man that made her bristle and want to step backwards to get out from his shadow.

His fitted black shirt covered a hard body and wide shoulders—but that was only part of it.

His blue eyes were the colour of forget-me-nots in the spring, and they contrasted so intensely against his deep suntan and heavy eyebrows that they seemed to be illuminated from within. And at the moment those eyes were focused totally on her. Light from the large picture windows in the restaurant shone on one side of his face, throwing his long shapely nose and square jaw into sharp profile.

If it was not for the thin white scar that cut through one of his eyebrows, and the dark bruise of shadows under his eyes, she would have said that he was gorgeous.

But she would settle for the upper end of the handsome scale.

Overall, he was probably the most masculine man she had met in a very, very long time. Not that she met many male customers in a life that whirled between Tara's flat and the kitchen they used for their catering business.

He took a step away from her and released her arms. She inhaled the scent of cheese and lunch, good bread and...chocolate. Not the full-cream praline chocolate she had used to make the dessert he had just enjoyed, judging from the clean dessert plates, but an undercurrent of bitter, sharp and aromatic cocoa. As distinctive as any type of coffee or wine. And, to her attuned senses, as tantalising as the most expensive cologne any Paris perfumier could concoct.

That was probably why her throat went amazingly dry the instant one side of his mouth turned up into a cheeky smile which creased the side of his face and was obviously intended to make her swoon at his charm.

Not going to happen.

Even if it was remarkably effective. And he still smelt amazing.

She flicked her hair back behind one ear, desperate for something to do whilst attempting to find out why he had called to her. Perhaps his lovely wife had sent him to apologise, and he was being a dutiful husband?

Then she looked into his eyes.

Okay. Perhaps not such a good boy after all.

In fact those eyes were sparkling with excitement, and an interest which seemed to be aimed at her.

A frisson of more than professional interest lit like a fuse inside her poor heart—before she dumped a large bucket of icy water over it.

This was a married man with a child, whose mother was still sitting in the retaurant! The sooner she remembered that and let him get back to his coffee and his elegant and stunningly beautiful wife the better.

Handsome people who had won first prize in the gene pool lottery belonged together—not in kitchens with the hired help.

Daisy lifted her chin. She had waved goodbye to being second best the day she'd packed her bags and left Paris and her cheating former boyfriend Pascal behind. Not even this Greek-god-handsome face and body were going to sway her down that rocky path again. She had learnt the hard way that good things did not always come in beautifully wrapped packages.

This man looked like a praline wrapped in gold foil, but for all she knew that tempting cover might well conceal a bitter lemon boiled sweet. All promises. No delivery. Been there, done that, and hadn't even come back with the T-shirt to show for it.

'Did you need something, Mr Ormandy?' she asked in as sweet a voice as she could manage—but the tone seemed to emerge as a sort of a squeak.

'I was hoping that you might spare me a few minutes to talk about a business proposition, Ms Flynn. And please call me Max, as all my friends do,' he murmured, and flashed her the full-on charming smile which, aimed at any other woman, would instantly have had her on her knees.

The cheek of the man! His wife was still in the same room, chatting to the head chef. She didn't know what kind of business proposition he had to offer her, but she knew she didn't want anything to do with it.

Even so, she had to rally her defences before replying.

'A business proposition? What kind of business could we possibly have in common? Unless, of course, you happen to be in the chocolate trade? That is the only way you could tempt me to take you seriously.'

She had intended him to take her question as a joke. After all, she wasn't interested in the least in whatever he had to offer.

This was why his reply hit Daisy right between the eyes and rendered her completely speechless.

'Actually, I *am* in the chocolate trade. I happen to own an organic cocoa plantation in St Lucia. The Treveleyn Estate grows some of the finest organic cocoa beans in the world, and I'm looking for a dessert chef who is as passionate about chocolate as I am. Tempted now?'

CHAPTER THREE

'HAVE you ever heard of the Federation of Organic Cocoa Growers?'

Daisy looked at Max over the rim of her coffee cup and gave a quick nod of affirmation. They had escaped to a quiet corner of the restaurant while the waiting staff cleared the room after the end of the lunch service, but she was pleased that she was not alone with Max—especially since his lovely wife had already waved him goodbye and headed off towards the shops, leaving them to talk chocolate.

Chocolate. That was what she had to focus on. Not the way his blue eyes looked at her with such intensity that they seemed to glow.

He wanted to talk to her about chocolate. She could do that all day.

'I buy most of my chocolate from a small Belgian company who source their raw cocoa paste from federation members.' She put down her coffee cup, but wrapped her fingers around the delicate china before speaking again. 'Why do you ask?'

Max shuffled forward in his seat and rested his elbows on the table as he stretched his arms out towards her, closing the gap between them and making her wriggle a little on her chair.

'Simply this,' he said. 'I've just flown back from St Lucia so that I can attend their annual conference. It's being hosted this year by a hotel chain who specialise in boutique eco-hotels in luxurious settings. Think Bali, Malaysia, Costa Rica and a few unspoilt sites across Europe. Their hotel in Cornwall was a working abbey until a few years ago—they were virtually self-contained. And organic.'

Daisy smiled and took another sip of coffee. 'Any conference about cocoa sounds wonderful to me. I do struggle to keep up with the latest news sometimes—especially at this time of the year. In fact Tara is expecting me back in the office to get ready for two hen parties and a wedding rehearsal buffet lunch. I wasn't joking about the wedding season, and there's lots of extra cooking to do.' She licked her lips and put down her cup. 'But that doesn't mean that I am not passionate about chocolate. I'm just busy.'

Max laid his hand over hers just as she started to stand, startling her with the gentleness of his touch and the pressure of unfamiliar skin against hers.

'That's good to hear,' he said. 'Because I haven't got to the really good bit yet. This is a conference with a difference.' He slid his hand away before she had a chance to say anything.

Daisy breathed out in exasperation and frowned at him, only to be met with a smile of such total confidence that she finally surrendered to her curiosity and slid back into her chair.

'Five minutes,' she replied, and made a thing of looking at her watch.

Almost instinctively she sensed Max move forward, just enough to make her want to shuffle back, but she fought it to finish off her coffee and lower the cup back into the saucer with a clatter.

'I don't want to be rude, but either you're on commission for the hotel chain or I'm missing something here. Last time I checked St Lucia was a Caribbean island with pretty spectacular scenery and a lovely coastline of its own. Has the wonderful world of the internet not reached your plantation yet? I'm sure it is much more economical to do business over the web these days. I certainly wouldn't want to waste my time at parties when I could be working.'

'You're quite right.' He nodded in acknowledgement. 'But I wasn't joking about having a business proposition. You are clearly just as passionate about your business as I am about mine. That is why I have an idea which could be of benefit to both of us.'

His fingers tapped for a few seconds on the table.

'Let me start by telling you why I have travelled thousands of miles to be here, Ms Flynn. Firstly, I have my daughter's birthday coming up—but you already know that.' He paused for a second to flash a laser beam smile which made her choke slightly on the dregs in her cup. 'What you may not know is that for the last twenty years or so every sack of cocoa beans leaving the Treveleyn Estate has been snapped up at market prices by one of the largest confectionery companies in Japan.'

He raised one hand and then the other as he spoke, so that each word seemed to be punctuated by the waggle or curve of his fingers.

'They want top-quality cocoa beans which they roast and process in-house, and they come to me to make that happen—which is good news for them and good news for me…as far as it goes.'

His hands dropped back down to the table. 'The problem is that even with premium pricing there is still not enough money coming into the estate to give the farmers who work there a decent income and provide a future for their families.'

He sat back and stretched out his long legs, but she could see the tension in the multiple creases on his forehead and in the muscles in his neck.

'When I bought the estate I made a commitment to the families who work for me that I would make it my business to trade the amazing product we grow for the best price. Since then I've been working to make that happen. With something new. And that is why I am back in England.' Max reached down inside his rucksack and pulled out a zipped plastic bag containing a large white plastic ice cream container. 'Two years ago we started roasting and processing some of the cocoa on the estate. It has taken a lot of hard work, but I finally think we are there.'

He waved the box and carefully undid the lid a little. The delicious, powerful aroma of freshly ground chocolate filled the space between them.

'This is only a small sample of the cocoa paste I made last week. My plantation specialises in rare and amazing varieties of cocoa bean—the kind of fine flavour which would give unique characteristics to any chocolate. Now I am looking for new buyers who can truly appreciate what fine chocolate from a single estate in the West Indies can taste like, smell like—feel like on your tongue when you eat it.'

His mouth twisted into a smile of pleasure and delight as he spoke the words, and Daisy sat mesmerised, tempted to take a closer look at the raw chocolate and yet holding back, just in case it truly was as remarkable as Max believed it to be.

'But there is a problem.' He bowed slightly in her direction. 'I want to sell this pure cocoa direct to chefs. And to me the best way of doing that is by showing the master chocolatiers at this conference just how terrific my cocoa can be in the hands of someone who has a passion for chocolate. In short, I need someone like you, Miss Flynn.'

Daisy blinked several times and stared at Max across the table. 'Why me? There are lots of dessert chefs in London who would love to try your chocolate if it is as good as you say it is.'

'I have just tasted a sample of your work. Believe me—my cocoa would be perfect for desserts like the one I have just eaten. Silken, perfumed and delicious. With just a hint of spice. I know that my chocolate and your recipes would be an amazing combination. In exchange you would, of course, be the first chef in the world to use artisan single-estate cocoa from the Treveleyn Estate. And all you have to do is agree to use my chocolate. What do you say? Are you willing to give it a try?'

Daisy's heart started thumping as the impact of what Max was suggesting hit home.

A new organic chocolate supplier from the West Indies was offering her a single-estate fine chocolate. This could be the final magical ingredient she had been looking for—that unique final piece of the huge jigsaw puzzle.

It had taken her three years to recover from her disappointment in Paris, and there was not a day that had gone by without her thinking about how she could take that final step. Her very own signature chocolate. If there was any chance at all of her opening a chocolate shop with her name above the door, then she needed something remarkable to give her a unique edge over the other competitors.

She had worked hard, studied hard, and she had spent month after month working on recipes she knew would succeed. And yet she still had not felt quite ready to make the leap to her own business—not without that very special extra factor that would make her stand out from the crowd.

She had been disappointed before, but this could be it—she had to give him a chance.

Otherwise she might never be able to open her own chocolate shop.

Perhaps this scruffy man who loved her chocolate cake was the very person who could make her dream come true?

Suddenly her brain caught up with her heart.

This all sounded too good to be true. Perfect strangers did *not* come up to you in restaurants and offer you luxury cocoa. She was doing it again—she was allowing her enthusiasm and desperation to take over.

Business head on. Business head on.

'Forgive me for asking, but before I answer that question I would like to know more about your cocoa plantation. There are some horror stories out there about chefs who have been let down by wonderful suppliers after they have spent months working on recipes. I need to know that you would be able to continue supplying the same quality product month after month, year after year. I hope that doesn't sound too insulting, but chefs have to rely on their suppliers, and I wouldn't want to put my name on the line and make a commitment only to be let down,' she said firmly.

His reply was an intense stare, followed by a thin-lipped smile in which both sides of his mouth lifted at the same time, creating deep folds either side of his cheekbones. It was an all-embracing smile that a girl might fall into and be lost. Strange how she could not look away.

'Okay,' he drawled in that odd, lilting half-American accent of his. 'I suppose that could happen. But this is not some passing fad. Far from it. I bought the estate a few years ago, but it has been in my family for as long as I can remember. In fact I spent the first half of my life on that estate on St Lucia. My parents fell in love with the place, and the people, and so have I.'

Max paused and looked out of the window for a few seconds before chuckling to himself.

'The estate is a jealous mistress—but what can I tell you? I know every inch of her. I know where each variety of cocoa grows best, the microclimates around each river valley and native forest, and the names of every one of my estate worker's families.'

He turned back to Daisy, his brow furrowed

and intense, and when he spoke again each word seemed to echo inside Daisy's skull.

'I have invested everything I have in the future of the estate. And that's why the Treveleyn Estate will always deliver. You have my word on that, Miss Flynn.'

Daisy inhaled two deep breaths, and then pushed her coffee cup to one side with both hands, breaking the tension which had built up in that space between them.

The power in those simple words was so energising that his intensity and sincerity seemed to leap across the small table, grab her physically by the shoulders and give her a shake. He meant it. He was not simply managing this estate—it was his life.

It wasn't often that she met people with such a burning commitment and joy and drive for what they did—but she saw it in the man sitting across the table from her. Max Treveleyn was the real deal. He wanted to make a difference and do it on his own terms. And she admired him for that.

Her mind jumped from option to option, trying to weigh up the risks.

Should she take a chance? Take a chance on his passion? Or go through life settling for second best, just like her dad had done all of his life? Always waiting for his ship to come in. His bus to arrive. Waiting, waiting. Until it was finally too late to realise his dreams.

No. Never again. She was done with compromising. This could be precisely what she had been looking for. Even if Max Treveleyn was more like a Formula One racing car than a double decker London bus.

So she licked her lips, just once, and dared to look up at him with a faint smile, only too aware that his gaze had never once left her face.

'As it happens, I am always looking for new suppliers of fine organic chocolate which could give my restaurant dessert ranges that special edge.'

She immediately raised both hands, palms facing Max, as he half rose out of his chair with a great roar of triumph which sent the waiters scurrying away.

'No promises,' she said quickly, leaning back, startled. 'I have worked hard to make a name for myself. I shall need a price list and samples,

but—yes.' She nodded. 'I will give your chocolate a try.' She lowered her hands. 'I should be
able to get back to you in two or three weeks.'

The smile on Max's face broadened. 'Actually
my timeline is a little tighter than that.
Remember the conference I have just been telling you about? It happens to be running a very
special contest over the conference weekend.
With a prize you might be interested in.'

Daisy watched, mesmerised, as he reached
into his rucksack and pulled out a printed sheet
of paper with the logo of a famous hotel in green
as its header.

She stretched her neck high to try and read the
flyer, aware that Max was looking at her with
the kind of focus that was starting to make her
squirm. His blue eyes seemed startlingly bright
in the dim light in this quiet part of the restaurant, below dark blond eyebrows which were
broad streaks painted on his suntanned face.
They were so close that she could see his long
eyelashes were not black but dark brown. She
thought wryly that any girl would have been
grateful to have such long, full eyelashes, which
perfectly framed those stunning blue eyes.

'The idea is that each of the cocoa growers uses the organic chocolate they produce to cook three different dessert dishes from scratch in the hotel kitchens, under the beady eyes of the contest judges. The winners are announced at the end-of-conference gala dinner.'

Max grinned, displaying pearl-white teeth against his tanned face.

'It's chocolate lovers' heaven. Ambrosia from the gods. I would love to do it—except that until today I didn't have a dessert chef who was up to the task. Now perhaps I do. All you have to do is agree to cook a few desserts on Saturday. I can even pick you up on Friday and drive us down there. Simple!'

He waited for Daisy to reply. But there was only a stunned silence as she opened her mouth to speak, then closed it again.

'Oh, I know,' Max said, and rubbed his hands in glee and positively joggled in his chair. 'I can hardly wait for the sumptuous feast to begin.' Then his smile dropped. 'Miss Flynn? Where are you going?'

Daisy pushed her chair back and gave Max a short bow from the waist.

'Thank you for thinking of me. I'm not sure of your selection criteria, but I am flattered all the same—even if my answer is no. A contest like that would take months to plan, well in advance, which is what the other growers will have done. Unless, of course…' Daisy pressed both of her palms flat on the table as she stood up. 'You have already approached other chefs and they've turned you down. Is that it?'

Max stuck out his lower lip. 'I won't deny it. I did ask a few of my friends for recommendations. But strangely, all of those dessert chefs I telephoned seemed to be busy this weekend. Or had some other convincing excuse why they wouldn't take a risk with a small independent grower with a small plantation on a small island, even if I did wave several sacks of criollo cocoa beans under those noses.'

'Aha!' she exclaimed. 'Now things have started to become clearer. You've trawled your idea around every dessert chef in town and no one wants to work with you.'

Daisy stood up to her full height and glared at him. 'I don't know whether to be insulted by the fact that I'm a last-minute stand-in, or delighted that you happened upon my food stall this morning and now we have had this most entertaining chat. Lovely to meet you, Max. Best of luck!'

'Would it make any difference if I told you about the rather special prize the hotel chain is offering to the winner of this contest?' he said hurriedly.

'It would have to be spectacular to interest me—not merely special,' Daisy replied with a flick of her hair.

'How about a one-year contract to supply handmade chocolates to the entire hotel chain around the world? You would be expected to travel to promote the chocolates, and do a few demonstrations. But we are talking international first-class travel, and the finest and freshest organic ingredients from hand-picked growers and beautiful estates. Your name would be on every box of chocolates they sell or serve to their guests, and of course the hotel would pay for a full publicity campaign—giving you the kind of prestige marketing that money cannot buy.'

Max paused, then waggled his right hand in the air.

'Oh—and a five-figure cash prize to be split between the grower and the chocolatier. Just as an extra incentive.' He looked at her through his long dark brown eyelashes and smiled, so that creases crinkled in the corners of his eyes. 'All you have to do is work with me for four days at the end of this week. With your talent and my chocolate how could we lose?' he asked, in a voice as seductive and warm and smooth as the finest melted chocolate and cream sauce.

Daisy inhaled through her nose and tried to calm her racing Irish temper.

A contest at an international conference of cocoa growers!

This man had clearly not the faintest idea about how much work would be involved in putting together a range of recipes fit for a specialist conference in a five star hotel. The standard would have to be stellar.

Of course she wanted the marketing and publicity that the hotel chain could afford, and the cash prize was precisely what she needed to show the bank that she was serious and had some capital behind her, but even to have a chance in this contest she would need a huge investment of time and energy—and she only had a few days to make it happen!

There simply wasn't time to get ready.

She could not risk damaging her rising reputation by being ill-prepared for a contest in which the judges were probably going to be master chocolatiers—could she?

A clatter from the kitchen at the other side of the restaurant brought her back to the real world. She had just been offered a proper job by Marco, in the restaurant. She didn't want to work for anyone else, but Marco was offering her a great opportunity—instead of fairytale ideas of winning prestigious chocolatier contests.

'You have gone very quiet,' Max said, and bent down slightly so that he could look up into her face. 'Stunned? Excited?'

It was no good. Max was like a large, gorgeous puppy which bounded around the house full of beans, dragging goodness knew what onto the carpet, but no one could be angry with him because that was who he was. And there was no changing him.

'I am very sorry, but there simply is not enough time to prepare for a contest next weekend. I would be letting both of us down if I agreed to do it.'

She took a breath, only too aware that his boyish grin had been replaced by a look which screamed out disappointment. But she could not let that sway her. Even if he *did* look utterly dejected.

That was probably why she started babbling—just to fill the awkward silence with the sound of her voice.

'The truth is I don't want to work for a hotel chain full-time. My dream is to open my own artisan chocolate shop, under my own name, working for myself and creating the things I am passionate about. What you're suggesting is something completely different. I'm sorry, but I'm not the chocolatier for you. I am sure you will find someone else who is perfect for this contest,' she told him.

She smiled and stretched out her right hand. Max wrapped his long, tanned fingers around her small hand and gently squeezed it. His skin was warm, and she could sense the calluses on

the palm of his hand. It was the hand of someone who worked on the land—rough-skinned,
with broken cuticles and nails—it was an honest hand, and she paused just too long before
sliding her fingers from his.

'Will you at least think about it?' He reached
into the pocket of his trousers and picked out
a grubby business card from his wallet. 'Oh—
and don't forget your sample.'

He passed it to her, and was just about to
speak again when his cell phone rang. He instantly checked the caller identity. 'Oh, excuse
me. I need to take this. Apologies.'

Daisy stepped back from the table. She was
about to plunge her hands deep into the side
pockets of her chef's trousers when she noticed
that the lid was still open on the plastic box of
cocoa paste that Max had produced from his
bottomless rucksack. As she clicked it closed a
blob of raw cocoa slid down the side of the box.
Totally instinctively, and without even thinking about what she was doing, she scooped up
the piece of cocoa mass on her fingertip and
popped it into her mouth.

She almost reeled at the explosion of flavour

and aroma and utter bliss that bombarded her tastebuds with such power that she had to hang on to the table as her mind tried to process the sensory overload in the firework display that was happening inside her mouth.

She closed her eyes and revelled in the exquisite delight of the most remarkable chocolate she had ever tasted in her life. No added sugar or vanilla—just pure, one hundred per cent unadulterated pleasure. It was almost too much for her to take in. Her brain was already whizzing through her list of recipes, seeking out anything that could cope with flavours so intense and overpowering and coming up with dozens. This was not simply an ingredient. It was amazing. If one tiny taste had given her that kind of rush...Treveleyn Estate cocoa was better than sex. There would be girls all over England walking around with smiles on their faces if this stuff got out onto the market.

'I do have one question,' she finally managed to whisper as Max strolled back to the table after finishing his call.

'Go on.'

'Why on earth didn't you force this down my throat before? I have just changed my mind. I'll do it. I *will* go to this conference and I *will* cook up a storm and I *will* win. For both of us. Now, when would you like to start work? Because there is a lot to do and not much time to do it in. Oh—and you can call me Daisy if you like, Mr Ormandy.'

She picked up the plastic box and stared at it. 'This is…truly astonishing.'

Max was just standing there. Watching her. Grinning with delight.

'Well, at last we agree on something. And, seeing as we are going to be working together, you should know that Ormandy is Kate's maiden name. She decided to go back to it after we divorced. So please allow me to introduce myself.' He bowed slightly from the waist. 'Charles Maximilian Treveleyn, at your service. But, as I've already said, please call me Max.' He flashed her that grin again. 'Can you be at my place first thing Wednesday morning?'

* * *

An hour later Max was dealing with another troublesome female.

'Come on, Daddy. We are going to be *so* late.' Freya sighed with an exaggerated *humph*.

Max held on tightly to her tiny hand and pretended to be dragged along as they skipped across the road between the parked cars in the exclusive London suburb where Kate lived, then laughed down at her once they were safe on the pavement.

'Hey, what's all the rush for? Ashamed to be seen out with your old dad in public? Is that it? If you like I can take my jacket off and wear it as a hat. Or maybe carry you over my shoulder? Would that make it better?'

'No. Silly Daddy. My TV programme starts in ten whole minutes.'

Freya giggled as Max deliberately took smaller and slower steps. Just to prolong these precious few minutes when he was a real dad, picking up his daughter from school, and not just some tourist who breezed into her life every so now and then. Because no matter how often they spoke on the phone this was the real thing.

He glanced down at her as they slowed outside

a cake shop. Freya had inherited her mother's lovely blonde hair and button nose and fine features, but those blue eyes which were currently ogling the window display of horrendously expensive cupcakes were the same ones he looked at in the mirror. Some day, way too soon, that killer combination would be breaking boys' hearts.

Luckily for him, apparently there were also genes for greediness and a sweet tooth.

'Look, Daddy. Look! Mummy forgot to ask the man who brings the boxes from the supermarket for biscuits. Again. And Tracey will be coming over to play soon.'

Freya looked up and gestured with her hand for him to come down to her level so that she could whisper.

'I am going to have my party at the swimming pool. But you have to promise not to tell anybody, *ever*, because it is a totally *mega*-secret.' She pressed her forefinger to her lips for emphasis and made a loud shushing sound. '*It has to be a surprise.* But Tracey has to know because we have to plan what we are going to do and what we are going to wear and what games we are going to play and—oh, loads of stuff like that. It's so exciting that last night I kept waking up, thinking of all the things that we could do. It was amazing. And cool.'

Max nodded seriously. 'Not a word,' he said, and used his right finger and thumb to run a pretend zipper across his mouth, then twisted an imaginary button in the middle. He narrowed his eyes and looked to the right and then to the left, then back into her wide blue eyes. 'I hope that you haven't forgotten the most important thing?'

'What's that?' Freya asked in a hushed excited squeak.

'The chocolate rabbits, of course,' Max teased, and then clapped his hand over his mouth.

Freya rolled her eyes and took a tighter hold of his hand. 'I had those when I was, like, five. We don't *do* chocolate rabbits any more, Daddy.'

'You don't?' He blinked. 'How about ice cream with sprinkles? Or homemade cupcakes? Or doughnuts with cream and jam and icing and all kinds of gooeyness squishing out from the sides? Do you do them?'

She nodded furiously, and licked her lips and rubbed her tummy at the same time.

'Well, in that case we had better make a start on the baking—but how about we take a few of those cakes in the window home to practise on first?'

He did not have to say it twice, and Freya leapt into the shop, completely unaware of the heartache she left in her wake.

He would have liked to celebrate Freya's birthday at his cottage, with just the two of them, over a supermarket birthday cake and fizzy lemonade on the patio, instead of at the elaborate birthday party Kate was planning in London. According to the latest report, professional swim coaches, entertainers and a catering company were involved.

And that was what Freya wanted. It would have been cruel to take it away from her. She was so excited about the one and only time she would celebrate turning eight in her life.

She didn't want just her silly old dad and a couple of birds' nests and plants to look at in the cottage. Nor his chocolate bunnies, nor his hand-carved parrots and not his life.

His little girl was growing up and away from him.

His heavy lunch turned and growled inside his stomach. It was still early days yet, but the signs were all there. Would there come a day when she did not want him to pick her up from school because in her eyes her dad was a loser? A dreamer who had made his life on an island with some foolish dream of selling organic cocoa beans for a profit? A dad who was not there for her when she needed him? A dad who had let her down?

He waved at her little face as it grinned from inside the shop.

He had to make this estate a success. He had to. For her sake as well as his own.

CHAPTER FOUR

'YOU have *got* to be kidding me.'

'I know. It does look a little unassuming. But you can't deny it is close to home.'

Daisy pressed her lips together and blinked at the long thin building which took up almost the full length of the bottom part of the country garden. Hidden on the other side of a hedge, it was almost invisible from the pretty thatched cottage which Max called home—which was probably a good thing, because this brick monstrosity was one of the ugliest buildings she had seen in a long time. And she delivered to cafés all over London!

But this—this was something else.

Ivy grew out of the guttering and pigeons called to her from the tall trees almost touching the sloping metal roof, which was covered in splats of what pigeons did best.

The address that Max had scribbled down on

the back of a restaurant menu had seemed at first just like any other location, with a house number and a street and the name of a village in block capitals, just in case she got lost, but it had taken her almost an hour to drive from the city that hot Wednesday morning, and for the last ten miles she had barely exceeded twenty miles an hour. Winding narrow country lanes had led to villages with names like Nately Broomwood and houses called Badger's Tail Cottage.

And she *had* got lost. Twice.

Only her pride had prevented her from ringing Max and asking for directions. She had resorted to thumping the steering wheel and peering at her map of rural Hampshire instead. By the time she had found the cottage, down a remote country lane, her hair had been frizzed, her print sundress creased beyond repair and her special occasion sandals had been biting into her swollen feet.

Which went some way to explaining why she was now hot, sticky and tired, and the longer she stood in the heat the more exasperated and cranky she became.

Max Treveleyn, on the other hand, seemed

totally impervious to the hot weather. He was wearing a short-sleeved T-shirt promoting a long-defunct rock band and loose cotton work trousers which had dropped a couple of inches onto his taut round hips to expose the top of black boxers.

There was a smudge of dirt down one side of his long straight nose, the sun-bleached hairs on his tanned arms were grubby with grease, he had not shaved, and his hair was set with trails of cobwebs. His body temperature might be set to normal for a man used to the Caribbean, but to Daisy he still looked hotter than a hot thing from hot land, with a big dollop of hot and gorgeous on the side.

Which was more than a little annoying, considering how bedraggled she was feeling.

'It's a garage, Max. I was hoping for stainless steel and air-conditioning. And please tell me that you don't actually *make* the chocolate here. Food standards? Hygiene? People are very picky about that sort of thing in this part of the world,' she grumbled.

'Ah—to *you* it is a simple garage,' Max replied with a broad sweep of his right arm, totally unaware that he displayed a remarkable bicep at the same time. 'But to me it is the manufacturing powerhouse of the entire Treveleyn cocoa empire. And you haven't seen the best part. Come on inside. That is where the magic happens.' He waggled his eyebrows up and down several times, then gestured with his head towards a solid metal door. 'You wouldn't want to miss that.'

Stifling a groan, Daisy flashed Max an eyeroll, then stepped through as he held the door open for her. She stood to one side and took in the long, airy room.

Much to her surprise, the space was cool, clean and tidy, and apart from a few cobwebs in the corner of the ceiling, and a very musty smell, quite serviceable.

She had seen a lot of kitchens worse than this over the years.

Max had converted the brick shell of a very basic garage into a chocolate workshop by covering up the interior brickwork with generous applications of white paint and installing one long kitchen worktop which ran the full length of the far side of the room below double glazed windows. A smooth cement flooring soaked up what heat penetrated the white false ceiling, which was bright with halogen lights.

Sacks of cocoa beans and large plastic tubs were lined up on metal racking against one wall, and Daisy could make out a refrigerator at one side and various pieces of catering equipment covered in clear sheeting. But the centre of the room was dominated by a monster stainless steel mixing unit.

'Isn't she a beauty?' Max asked, as he whisked away the covers like a magician demonstrating his latest conjuring trick. He stood with a hand on each hip, grinning at the mixer as though they were looking at some stunning example of Italian motor engineering. 'Top of the range. I picked it up at a great price from a small Belgian company that had been bought out by one of the big firms.' He rubbed the palms of his hands together in delight. 'I can't wait to see the old girl in action at long last.'

At long last? Oh, no...

'Please tell me that you have used this machine before?' Daisy asked with a whimper.

'Nope,' Max replied. 'I was waiting for the perfect occasion—and this is it.'

Daisy stared at the shiny steel behemoth, then chuckled to herself and shrugged as a totally silly idea popped into her head. 'I bet you have even considered giving your mixer a pet name.' She glanced up at Max, who was still stroking the metal cover. There was a slight tension around his eyes that made her gasp. 'Oh, no, please—not that. You *have*, haven't you?'

'Dolores is a perfectly respectable name for a lovely piece of engineering which is going to make our fortune.'

'Dolores?'

Max patted the mixing bowl. 'Dolores, meet Daisy. This is her first time at the cottage, so I need you to be on your very best behaviour. Just for me. Okay?'

Daisy closed her eyes for a second, and fought down a very unkind comment about boys and their toys. Because Dolores was not a toy. Far from it. Dolores was going to have to work first time or there simply wouldn't be any chocolate. And if she did not have any chocolate to work with, then there would not be a contest.

'Nice to meet you, Dolores. It's good to have you on the team.' Daisy smiled through half gritted teeth. This was what she had been reduced to—she was talking to inanimate objects.

'Excellent,' Max replied, rubbing the palms of his hands together again. 'Team Treveleyn. I like the sound of that.'

With an athletic spin on his heels, Max turned to Daisy and gestured towards the carefully labelled large white tubs on the worktop. 'I have everything you need. I have my cocoa paste, I have cocoa butter, I have vanilla and organic sugar, and a whole range of gorgeous extras in the fridge in the corner over there. So just say the word and Dolores and I will spring into action. Your wish is my command.'

He smiled at her with all the energy and enthusiasm of a teenager high on sugar and additives. His eyes were gleaming with an expression of such infectious excitement and happiness that she could feel his energy from across the other side of the mixing bowl.

'We can't wait to get started on my first commercial batch of Treveleyn Estate chocolate. All you have to do now is tell me what the recipe is, and my lovely Dolores here will show us what she can do.'

Something close to a playful giggle threatened to bubble up inside Daisy, but she covered it with a quick cough. Because her brain had finally caught up with what Max had just told her.

'Wait. I don't understand. Did you just say that this was your first batch? You mean your first batch using Dolores or...?'

When he didn't reply, Daisy became aware that her mouth had half fallen open, but she simply couldn't help it.

'No. You *can't* mean to say that this is the first batch of chocolate that you have ever made?' she asked with horror.

'Of course.' Max shrugged. 'Oh, I have seen it done dozens of times at other estates where they make their own couverture, but not me. I have been holding back for the right time and the right opportunity. Why else would I drag you all the way from London? This is going to be a first for both of us.' He frowned. 'Didn't I mention that part?'

Daisy closed her eyes and tried the deep breathing exercises her assertiveness training evening classes had suggested. They had never worked before, but it was worth a try.

You see? This is what happens when you are swayed by a handsome face waving amazing cocoa under your nose.

Duped.

Sold down the river.

Taken for granted by yet another hunkalicious fella who thinks you are going to be putty in his hands.

Again.

'Not to worry,' Max said with a smile in his voice. 'It will be fine. How about a cold drink before we get started? I think I must have eaten all the biscuits last night, but the village shop might still be open.'

Nope. Still not working.

She slowly creaked open her eyes to find that Max had slid over next to her and was bending over from the waist to peer at the contents of the refrigerator. His tight, delicious bottom was pushed back, so that his scratchy trousers were low on his hips, and the rough fabric brushed against her bare legs as he tugged two cans of fizzy orange drink from the bottom shelf. To her horror, a shiver of delicious pleasure quivered through her traitorous body.

Oh, no—she was *so* not going to that place. Especially not now she knew that she had pinned her hopes on a dreamer with delusions of grandeur.

Max was a charming, attractive, passionate man who produced wonderful cocoa. But he was a dreamer all the same.

Normally she liked dreamers. She had to. She was one herself. But right now, at this moment, the futility of what she was trying to achieve hit her hard—then hit her again like the cold draught from the refrigerator as Max stood back to his full height. There was a time and a place for dreams—but this was not it.

'Actually,' she murmured through clenched teeth, 'there are a few things that you forgot to tell me when you suggested that I drive down here for a...how did you describe it? Oh, yes. A planning meeting. *Planning.* Yes, that was the word you used.'

She pivoted around to face him, one hand flat on the worktop, the other pointing very rudely towards his chest, and stared hard into his rather startled eyes.

'Not once did you mention the fact that you still have to actually *make* the chocolate I need in three days.' Daisy paused and blinked several times. 'Which actually makes my head hurt just thinking about it. Have you *any* idea of how much work there is going to be involved? The mixing time is crucial. I have no clue whether you are going to need nine hours or nineteen, and it all depends on the level of cocoa butter, and…oh, about ten other factors which all need to come together to make something worth eating.'

She closed her eyes and took a deep breath, because her heart was thumping too loudly for her to hear her own thoughts.

In a second she felt strong fingers pressed around her bare elbow and the sound of a plastic garden chair being pulled out from under the worktop.

Before she could complain, or fully register what was happening, Daisy felt the chair against the back of her knees and that was it.

She was sitting down. Weight off her feet. Cool and comfortable.

It was such a relief that she sighed out loud and sat back in a slump.

'Hot day. Do I need to find you a glass?' Max asked as he ripped the tab from the can.

The icy-cold can of drink was passed into her hand, and Daisy greedily drank down several mouthfuls of fizz and artificial colours and sweeteners.

'That's fine, thanks,' she replied, then took a moment for her heart to slow down.

'I know what you're thinking,' Max said, as he drained the entire can and stretched out on another chair. 'Rest assured. Freya doesn't know that I keep my secret stash of contraband junk food in here. Adults only.'

Daisy exhaled very slowly, her eyes firmly fixed on the mixer, before taking another long drink. 'That wasn't exactly what I was thinking,' she admitted, and lifted her chin towards Dolores.

Max shuffled forward in silence and she could see his legs stretched out in front of him—so that both of them were talking to Dolores instead of one another.

'Ah. I see. You know, I have been working with the same team on the estate all my life. They know me and I know them. As a result it would seem that my communication skills and my assumption that you can mind-read leave something to be desired. Sorry. I shall try to do better going forward.'

'Are we going forward?' Daisy asked in as calm a voice as she could muster as she turned her head to look at him.

Max lifted his can and toasted her.

'I hope so. Yes, I *do* still have to make the chocolate. But I was under the impression that a master chocolatier like yourself would bring her own recipe for the perfect blend of cocoa and other fine ingredients. I would be wasting my time and my cocoa in producing something which was not up to your exemplary standards. Hence the long mixing time. But—' he crunched his drink can flat with one squeeze '—I can understand it if you would prefer to spend the evening with your boyfriend in London, instead of blending chocolate with a crazy and deluded amateur.'

His eyes seemed to scan her face so intently that she could not stand it a moment longer and slipped out of her chair to walk the few steps to the steel sink unit. She swallowed down the remains of her drink to soothe her throat, before running cold water over the insides of her wrists.

He was offering her the chance to create her very own blend of chocolate.

It had never even occurred to her that it was an option.

It was the golden prize she had always wanted but had held back from until she had a shop like Barone where she had trained in Paris, which was large enough to justify the expense of special equipment.

She was an idiot. Max was treating her like a pro and all she could do was complain.

It was rare that she met someone who worked with chocolate at this level, and she had become accustomed to being treated as just another dessert chef instead of a highly trained chocolatier.

Even Marco did not expect her to mix her own chocolate blend.

How pathetic was that? She should be ashamed.

Only then was she finally ready to twist back to face Max and answer him.

She was standing, pressed against the sink. He was sitting, half turned in his chair, so that his head was about the same height as her chest.

'Okay.'

'Okay?' he said, with a lilting question in his voice.

She nodded. 'Okay. I may not have a boyfriend waiting for me back in London, tonight or any other night, but I *do* have a family recipe for the chocolate I have always wanted to make. I have been waiting three years to have the chance to see if it tastes as delicious as I hope it will.'

Daisy reached into her bag, found her wallet, and slowly pulled out a crushed single piece of paper. Her fingers held onto the precious note as though they were reluctant to hand it over to someone she barely knew. There was so much history associated with this single page. So many faded dreams and lost opportunities.

Max was giving her the opportunity to do something she had been looking forward to for a very long time.

But could she trust him with her hopes and dreams?

She looked into his face and swallowed down her apprehension before passing the paper to him. 'I have been carrying this around with me for years. Waiting for the day when I could finally find out if it would work. Or not. For that I am willing to give you a chance. Do not let me down, Max. I mean it. Okay?'

Max stood up, stretched out his arms, and for a terrible, wonderful moment she thought that he was going to hug her. But he simply laid his hands on her arms for a fleeting second, leant forward, and pressed his lips to her cheek in a kiss which was so warm and sweet and genuine that the joy simply beamed out of him—as though he was reflecting the sun streaming in through the window that was warming Daisy's back.

'You are a star, Daisy Flynn. And you won't

regret your decision for a moment. Because we are going to make a chocolate so stunning that the world will be beating a path to our door! You wait and see. Let me get changed and I'll be right back. Do not move an inch.'

He released her arms so quickly that she slipped back against the cool sink, simply watching him bound the few steps to the door, and then he was gone, leaving a trail of dust in his wake.

Her cheek and her arms were tingling. Her throat was dry and her mind was buzzing.

One kiss on the cheek and she was mush.

Her no touching rule was going to be a lot harder to adhere to than she had expected.

What had she let herself in for?

For once Daisy was grateful that she did not have long fingernails, because the process of loading up the mixer had taken so long that they would have been bitten down to nothing by now.

In the end all she could do now was watch the still untidy cocoa farmer fiddle with the controls and hope and pray that he knew what he was doing. At least he looked the part. Max had swept his long blond hair back under a bandana and taken the time to scrub his hands and fingernails before working with the ingredients.

All she had been able to do was clean the equipment and assemble everything they needed.

At long last Max wiggled his fingers in the air and passed them from side to side over the large steel mixing vessel. 'Let me check that we haven't missed anything. My cocoa paste. Vanilla. Lecithin. A little sugar and spice. And, last but not least, the precise quantity of cocoa butter to meet *madame*'s exacting standards for her very special dessert chocolate. I think it is time to actually melt this chocolate. What do you say? That way we can make a start on the tempering and actual cooking in the morning.'

Daisy bit her lower lip, and then nodded. Twice. Quickly. It had taken almost an hour to weigh everything out, but the mixture already smelled totally amazing.

She quickly double-scanned the list, then popped it back into her pocket. 'Let's do it. I only hope that it tastes as good as it smells.

Fantastic. Fruity. Smooth, but with a definite spiciness to it. I love it already.'

She shrugged her shoulders high, and then wiggled them a little in sheer joy, making Max splutter.

'I didn't say a word,' he said in a deliberately calm voice, his eyebrows lifted and chin high. Then his whole face relaxed in approval. 'It's lovely to see someone who is just as excited as I am. And this is a first for me too, remember?'

Daisy sucked in a breath. 'Dolores does look rather…well, complicated. Do you have an instruction booklet? I find them ever so helpful.'

Max replied with a dismissive snort. 'My Dolores is a high-class girl, but I know how to flick her switches—if you know what I mean.' He pointed to the simple control panel above the water bath. 'Two buttons. On and off. And the speed dial. Looks easy enough.' His eyes sparkled with exhilaration and excitement and he gestured with his head towards the mixer. 'Ready to find out just how fantastic this chocolate is going to taste?'

This was an important moment. She did not

want to spoil a life-changing event by petty squabbling about the mixer settings.

So, instead of following her instincts and starting off cautiously, Daisy shrugged off her concerns and stepped closer, buoyed up by his energy and enthusiasm.

With one single nod in her direction Max turned to the machine, pressed the 'on' button and set the speed to its lowest setting.

To Daisy's delight green lights appeared on the control panel and the blades inside the warm chocolate started moving, mixing and smoothing away any grittiness from the cocoa butter inside the blend. *Yes!* This was it.

Her first batch of her very own recipe.

'Oh, this is so fantastic. Thank you, Max. I have waited a long time for this moment.'

'Me too,' he replied in a low, warm voice, and opened up his arms to receive her.

It seemed natural and right for Daisy to step inside the circle of his embrace and press her chest against his. His arms wrapped around her in a bear hug, holding her tight against him. She sighed as she realised he was probably unaware that she had closed her eyes and was simply revelling in the physical contact.

She could feel his heart beating just below the thin fabric of his loose T-shirt, and when he suddenly chuckled the echoes of his laugher reverberated through his chest into hers, making her feel young and foolish and naïve and happy again. As though she were just starting out on her great adventure all over again.

It was a wondrous, joyous feeling that she wanted to hang on to as long as possible. Here inside Max's arms she felt that she could do anything in life she wanted.

He was holding her so tightly against him that her arms automatically lifted around his neck, and as her fingers meshed behind his neck Max lowered his head, so that their brows were almost touching.

Daisy breathed in a totally entrancing aroma of spicy sweet chocolate, man-sweat and exhilaration. It was a perfume as sensual and rich as any fragrance, which combined with the warm softness of his breath on her cheek and the rough rasp of his chin stubble on her forehead to create a total sensory overload for her poor exhausted brain.

This was one of those moments which came so rarely in her life that she knew it would stay with her long after Max had headed back to his island. The kind of moment when life could spin forward and, just for once, she would be helpless against the power of the sensation.

Little wonder that she gently shifted even closer against Max, so that their bodies were in contact from thigh to chest.

His lips pressed softly against her hair as he hugged her closer, his fingers wide and strong and powerful through the thin fabric of her dress as they hugged her so close that he almost lifted her off her feet.

It felt so good. Max felt so good.

She had almost forgotten what it was like to be held in the arms of a desirable man who seemed to be enjoying the moment just as much as she was.

Heat and physical pleasure surged up from deep in her stomach, prickling her skin and making her blood pound.

She could fight this attraction.

She *should* fight this attraction. Tell him to stop.

But as she lifted her chin to ask Max to put her down she made the mistake of looking into those blue eyes, and what she saw there made her gasp.

More than simply attraction. Desire. A slow-burning sensual desire to match the slow circles his hands were making on her back. His hug was turning into a caress.

And she liked it.

Taking a deep breath, throat dry and palms sweaty, Daisy steadied herself as Max started to lower his head towards hers. She licked her lips and was just about to angle her head to receive his kiss when the slow, regular paddle action of the mixing blades started to speed up and she heard a strange grinding, whining sound.

Max froze, then stared over at Dolores in alarm.

Her hands slid down from his neck onto his chest as he released her, and they both watched in horror as the mixing blades turned faster and faster, churning up the thin warm chocolate which started splashing up the sides of the mixer and onto the table.

'Max, isn't that a little...well, fast?'

'It is,' he answered, the crease in his forehead becoming even more pronounced. 'Problem is, according to the dial this is the lowest setting.' He reached forward before Daisy could stop him and spun the speed control dial to maximum. 'Perhaps the wiring on the dial is reversed? Only one way to find out.'

Except that his hand had barely left the dial before the mixer blades started rotating so fast that the chocolate was being thrown about into the air.

'No—turn it off. Turn it off!' Daisy gasped.

'I'm trying, but I think the switch is broken,' Max replied, diving to one side to avoid the deluge while desperately trying to fiddle with the speed controller.

Great splatters of warm molten dark brown chocolate blend hit Daisy on the neck, and then slid down the front of her dress. She instinctively raised her hands to protect her eyes from the spray, just as Max conceded defeat and switched off the power at the socket on the wall.

Too late. Her neck, shoulders and arms were covered.

There was a deathly hush in the room, broken only by the gentle plopping sound of chocolate dripping down from every surface it had collided with.

Daisy wiped away a blob of brown congealing mess and casually, slowly opened her eyes. She stood frozen in total awe at the devastation one large mixer full of molten chocolate could create. If Max had intended to decorate the old garage in a fetching shade of chocolate-brown he could not have done a better job.

Max was standing next to the power switch on the wall, his mouth open.

He looked at her.

She looked at him.

Then he licked his lips and used a fingertip to scoop some of the now cooling and congealed chocolate from his arm and taste it.

'Wow. Absolutely delicious. This is it. I think we have a winner. What do you think?'

'I think Dolores hates me. That is what I think. The minute you hugged me she went completely out of control.'

Daisy flicked her fingers out and droplets of molten chocolate flew off the ends, splattering the stainless steel table which was already half an inch thick in places.

A quick glance at her clothing confirmed that she was a mess, and her hands and skin were a mess, and as she took one step backwards it became apparent that the chocolate had dripped into her favourite sandals which she had bought in Paris.

She vaguely remembered hearing about some exclusive spa resort that used cocoa products as part of its beauty treatments and face masks. She had never seen the point of that. It was far better to *eat* chocolate and enjoy the benefits in a far more traditional fashion.

A feeling of total exasperation and madness bubbled up within her.

She had two choices. She could either see the positive side of being doused in chocolate and laugh at how ridiculous they both looked, which was what Max seemed to be doing. Or she could take stock of what she was doing in this crazy place, with this crazy man, with this crazy idea of entering a prestigious contest in a few days' time with some of the world's finest cocoa growers and chocolatiers.

Max might have a superb luxury ingredient. But what was she *doing* here?

How could she have been so stupid as to place her trust and her professional reputation in the hands of this…big kid?

This gorgeous, sexy, attractive big kid, whom she'd almost made the horrible mistake of kissing only a few minutes ago.

She groaned, and shook her head slowly from side to side.

She was tired, hungry, and her feet were squelching in chocolate. But she was grateful that Dolores had just saved her from doing something very, very stupid.

Daisy looked up at Max, who was standing with his hands on his hips, a huge grin on his face, as though this was the best fun in the world and he was right there at the centre of it.

In that moment she saw Max the teenager. The kind of boy who was a natural leader in sports events. The kind of boy who was always chosen to be captain of whatever club he decided to join. A boy who climbed trees for fun, scaled mountain peaks for the rush, and who would go anywhere and do anything if he was interested enough to apply himself to the task.

The kind of boy who would never, ever read an instruction manual.

Her brain screamed out that she was making a huge mistake and she should jump into her car and head back to London as fast as she could. While her heart totally warmed to the boyish charm and the adorable laughter lines that peeked out from below the sheen of chocolate on his nose and face. His laughter rang out and filled the room, melding with the intense aroma of chocolate in the warm afternoon sunlight streaming in through the side windows.

'Perhaps I should have supplied safety equipment,' he said, and shrugged, shaking his head as he looked around.

She could not believe it. She was doing it again. She was allowing another handsome man to blind her and divert from what she had set out to do.

Max was dazzling! But he was also responsible for all this mess.

In a few days he expected her to walk into a

professional conference where her reputation and his products would be on the line. Would he let her down when it came to the work? The preparation? The tedious background jobs she had always been assigned while the boss took the credit?

And what if they *did* win? Could she rely on him to produce the same quality cocoa beans year after year? This seemed to be some huge joke to Max—a great entertainment.

She had promised herself that she would never again make the same mistake she had made with her former boyfriend Pascal Barone in Paris. She wouldn't stake her future career on someone who was not as dedicated and passionate as she was. His uncle, Chef Barone, who actually owned Barone Fine Chocolate, was a master chocolatier who had poured his life into his work—but she had got it badly wrong when she'd assumed that his nephew Pascal felt the same.

And right now she was making exactly the same mistake with Max Treveleyn. Worse. She had almost kissed him.

He was laughing his head off when all their

morning's work and a huge amount of chocolate had been wasted.

Just like that her heart conceded defeat to the battering it was getting from the sensible part of her brain.

Stupid. That was what she was. A total, complete idiot.

Daisy ran her tongue over her lips and mouth and tasted chocolate. He was right. It *was* delicious—and would be even better given the correct mixing time and a couple of tweaks to the ingredients. But now they would have to start again from scratch and repeat the whole process.

She did not know whether to laugh or to cry.

So she told him the truth.

'Max?'

He looked up at her, and the smile lines on his face creased into dark chocolate smears which on his tanned skin looked tantalisingly good enough to lick off. She inhaled quickly and straightened her back.

'This is very good chocolate. And I know I could make spectacular products with it. But I need more than that. I need someone I can rely on—someone who takes his work seriously. Someone looking to the future. Someone who will keep on delivering cocoa of this quality.'

She slid her hands back from the table, so that only the fingertips were in contact with the metal surface. He was watching her in silence now, his mouth calm and straight, his hands resting on Dolores, but his eyes were on fire and it took an effort for her to say the final words she needed to get out.

'I'm sorry, Max, but this is not working out for me. You need to find another chef to work with.'

She stood back and brushed her hands together, adding flakes of half-dried chocolate to the mess on the worktop. 'Do you mind if I use your bathroom before I head back to London?'

CHAPTER FIVE

MAX opened the cold water tap to maximum, clenched both hands around the ceramic rim of the large square butler's sink, closed his eyes, and plunged his head under the stream of running water, bending his head from side to side so that the water cascaded down over his neck and shoulders.

His shoulders dropped forward, releasing the tension for a few minutes, before the chill worked its magic. Releasing his grasp on the sink, Max pushed his hands through his hair to try and rinse away the combined grime of a morning of hard work on the cottage blended with a thin layer of melted cocoa. As hair conditioners went, this one still had a long way to go.

Just like him.

Eyes blinking, Max threw back his shoulders and combed his wet hair backwards with his fingers, throwing out droplets over the stone kitchen floor and down his bare back.

Max glanced out of the large window above the sink. It was the only modern glazed window in the cottage, and his grandmother had used to love the view over the garden as she worked in the kitchen. Her window on the world, she'd used to call it. And she had been right. This *had* been her world.

But for a long time it had not been his. Far from it. But now he had to make the best of what he had. This cottage was the only piece of England that truly belonged to him—and Freya. It was her inheritance as much as it was his.

He frowned.

This was where he had hoped to spend a two-week summer holiday with Freya. Instead of which he would have to make do with a weekend visit following her birthday, before Kate whisked her off to a château in France. So that would probably be the last time he could spend time with Freya until Christmas, and this year was certain to be a lot different now that her mother was engaged. His little girl was going to have a new family—new people who were bound to fall in love with her and want her to be part of their lives.

The thought of sharing her was so hard he simply did not want to think about it.

Rolling his neck and shoulderblades, Max sniffed once and sighed out loud to ease away the deep tiredness that would so easily overwhelm him if he let it.

He had tossed and turned in bed most of the night, before surrendering at dawn to the killing combination of jet lag from his long, uncomfortable economy flight from St Lucia and Kate's news about her plans for Freya.

Max raked his fingers through his wet hair again and blew out very slowly as guilt hit him harder than usual. Freya needed him just as much as he needed her—and so did his farmers.

It never got easier to balance the two main responsibilities in his life. But he had already come close to losing his connection to Freya when he'd lost Kate. They had both worked hard to make sure that did not happen. But now Kate was getting married again.

No. He did not have time to indulge the deep pool of anxiety that had started to well at the pit of his stomach the moment Kate had told him that she was engaged.

Because, whether he liked it or not, Freya was going to share her life with a brand-new stepfather. Anton would be the one to kiss her scraped knees better and read her bedtime stories and hug her when she needed a hug. Anton would be the man helping her with her homework and cheering from the sidelines on sports day.

Suddenly Max flung open the kitchen door and stepped outside into the warm air, trying to calm his agitated breathing.

Things needed to change.

He needed to turn the estate around and build a solid financial future. Selling organic cocoa beans at premium rates would be a good start.

And now he had to find some way to persuade Daisy Flynn to see that he was *not* a complete idiot and that they *could* be ready in time for this contest.

She had driven all the way from London to work on their business—and in exchange he had done everything possible to demonstrate that he was a disaster.

What had happened in the mixing room had

been a mistake. He could see that now. The fact that she was the cutest thing in a pink sundress he had seen in a long time was totally irrelevant if she could not take him seriously. But those legs!

No. They had simply been caught up in the excitement of the moment. That was all. He had only imagined that she had wanted more just as much as he had.

But what more could he give her? They had only just met, for one thing. And anything else would be madness—he had already destroyed one relationship with his arrogant belief that he could do anything, work every hour of the day, and still have someone there waiting for him to come home. And like it. *Wrong.* He had become a cliché. A workaholic who loved his job more than anything else in the world. And vague excuses about it only being a temporary effort had stopped being credible as the months became years.

The estate was demanding and insatiable and always would be.

Max glanced across at a framed photograph of his parents, taken on St Lucia. They were standing in front of the plantation house—*his* house. They had given him everything he could want as a boy. The least he could do was honour them by keeping the plantation and their dream of an organic cocoa business alive.

And in the process make his daughter proud of her dad.

With that final thought, he roughly grabbed a sponge and headed out to the hosepipe.

Hot water cascaded down over Daisy's shoulders and she dipped her head back and rinsed her hair for the third time.

She loved chocolate. She truly did. But not as a bodywash.

It had taken three shampoos and a pink foam sponge she'd found in the bathroom cabinet to scrub away the final traces of brown gunge—delicious though it had been—from her skin.

Daisy wrapped herself in a bathsheet and demisted a space in the bathroom mirror.

A pink-faced, well-scrubbed girl stared back at her with a slightly startled expression.

Her hair was standing on end—as usual—and she did not hold out much hope for anything close to a hairbrush or a hairdryer. Not in *this* cottage!

Towelling herself dry, Daisy tugged on her underwear, which had survived relatively un-scathed, apart from a stain on her bra strap, be-fore wrapping the now moist towel back around herself to protect her modesty. Max had mur-mured something about washing in the kitchen, but she did not want to run into him semi-clad in the corridor.

Max.

Daisy sat down on the toilet seat and glared at the bathroom door as though it was a portal to a new world where anything might happen.

What was she going to do about Max?

He had barely said a word since she'd told him that she was leaving. More polite muttering than joined up intelligent sentences. He had simply pointed to the bathroom and the small spare bedroom before disappearing back towards the garden.

She rubbed her hands over her face. There was a huge mess waiting to be cleaned up in the workshop. And it would take hours to dis-mantle the equipment and wash and dry the components before he could even try to start a new batch of chocolate.

Guilt nagged at the corner of her soft heart.

Max had already paid the entrance fee for the conference contest, and booked her hotel room. Finding a replacement chocolate chef was not going to be easy at such short notice.

How could she recommend him to her friends in the trade when she was not prepared to give him a chance herself?

But perhaps it was better this way—Max was not ready to work with chocolate. He could still make an income for himself with the sales of the cocoa beans, and in the meantime he could build on his skills and read instruction manuals! Preferably before he powered Dolores up again.

Either way, she could not hide in the bathroom all day. It would be better for them both if she simply borrowed something to wear while her dress dried in the garden and drove back to London as soon as possible.

Then she could put all this behind her.

Put Max behind her. And his daughter Freya. And this lovely cottage and the amazing chocolate he made. And how wonderful it had felt to be in his arms for those precious fleeting moments in the garage.

Oh, no! She groaned and shook her head, before pressing the heel of her hand against her forehead.

How did she get herself into these situations?

What an idiot. Even *thinking* about staying on here was bound to lead to even more disaster in every way possible. What had she been thinking? Except, of course, thinking had not come into it at all.

Snap out of it, girl. She sniffed and stuck out her chin. She could do this. This was her decision. She had to thank Max for the offer but say this was not for her. Any of it. Especially the Max part.

Daisy cautiously opened the bathroom door and stepped out into the hall, which was strangely quiet. No running water. No howls of angry rage. No sign of Max.

Then she realised that something rather important was missing.

Her sandals! They were still outside in the garden, next to the hosepipe, and she would not leave without them.

In the meantime, her feet were freezing. Perhaps Freya's mother had left behind a pair of slippers she could borrow for a few minutes while her only pair of couture sandals dried off? Failing that, she would have to resort to the wet shoes. Or beg some socks from Max.

Daisy looked around the small, cosy and simply furnished cottage bedroom. With its low ceiling and solid timber beams it was a perfect bedroom that any little girl would love. The bedcover and curtains were made from a pretty floral fabric with butterflies and sprays of small flowers and a cream background. The plastered walls were painted in cream, and on one wall, opposite the bed, above a chest of drawers, was a collection of personal photographs.

Daisy stepped over to the framed photographs. Each one captured an image in Freya's life.

This was Max with his little family.

Max as a new father, gazing lovingly and with total astonishment into the face of the tiny baby a smiling Kate was holding in her arms while Max wrapped one protective arm around her shoulder. A little blonde girl in a yellow sundress running towards her father across the grass. Freya at school, birthday parties and Christmas celebrations.

Max truly did have a very pretty daughter who would be breaking hearts soon enough.

Daisy sat down on the bottom of Freya's bed and smiled up at the collection. Yes. This was exactly how she would want to wake up every morning. Looking at the happy faces of the people she loved and knowing that they loved her back just as much. Especially her father.

Daisy reached down and picked up a single pink sock from the bedroom rug. Her own mother had died when she was twelve, but it must be very hard for an eight-year-old to reconcile herself to the fact that her precious father was not going to be living in the same house or sharing her life on a day-to-day basis.

Her eyes scanned the wall of photographs.

The collection was very clever. Max wanted Freya to remember that he had been part of her life growing up and was still there for her now.

Daisy inhaled deeply through her nose and wondered if there was a similar wall of photographs of Freya in Max's bedroom. It must be so hard, leaving his little girl behind, knowing that he would not see her again for months at a time. And what had he said? Kate had a new fiancé?

Ouch.

Max Treveleyn might not be the greatest mechanical engineer in the world, but he was a good father. And yet he had sacrificed being with his daughter and possibly even his marriage to live on a plantation and grow the cocoa he was so passionate about.

He was loyal to Freya. She knew that much. And she admired that more than she could say.

She shook her head.

She might feel sorry for his situation, but that did not mean she should take a risk on him at this stage of her career. She was so close to her dream shop. If Max let them both down at the conference her reputation would be damaged in the small world of fine chocolate-making.

She blinked away a moment of weakness and, pushing off the bed, took the few steps to a slim wardrobe which stood to one side of the fireplace.

Tugging open the wardrobe door, she reached in to tuck the sock back inside—but instead stood transfixed. Because the wardrobe was full to bursting with children's clothing.

Ballet costumes with stiff pink and white tutu skirts. Party dresses, trousers and sweaters. Pyjamas and fluffy slippers in a tiny size—hats, scarves, jackets. It was wonderful—but it was also very private and special.

Max had saved these clothes for Freya to wear so that she would always feel comfortable when she stayed here.

It was totally magical.

Daisy swallowed down her sense of guilt that she had invaded this private space, closed the wardrobe door, and pressed her hand against it.

She remembered the time she'd come back from catering college to find her father had sorted out a wardrobe for her old clothes, all pressed and clean and ready for her to wear when she came home. She'd never told him that most of them were too small for her. She had just loved the idea that it had given him comfort to plan for her return when she was away.

And here was another father who had done the same.

Oh, Max.

Just like that her arguments about working with him seemed to fade into trivial gripes about his lack of technical skills. So he had bought a blending machine with a faulty speed control? That was hardly the end of the world.

And his chocolate *was* fantastic.

Maybe her decision to take off had been a little hasty. Maybe—just maybe—she could still make this work.

The heel of her right hand knocked several times against her forehead.

She was such a totally soppy girl. She was probably going to regret this. But she would give Max Treveleyn yet another chance.

But he had to understand why she was so serious about the work, or they would not stand a chance against the seasoned professionals at the conference.

With a huge sigh, Daisy stood up and peered at her reflection in the bedroom mirror. *Well? Are you going to do it or not?* she asked the girl with the crazy hair who was looking back at her. *Because you have to decide one way or the other. And you have to decide right now. You either go for it completely or you walk away now. No compromises.*

And absolutely, definitely, one hundred per-cent guaranteed no touching. At all. Ever again.

Ten minutes later, after much rummaging about in the cupboards in the hall, Daisy shuf-fled across the kitchen wearing a pair of foot-ball shorts and the smallest vest she could find, which still fell down over her hips.

She stepped outside the back door, looked around—then instantly froze, hardly believ-ing her own eyes. Transfixed.

Max was still scrubbing down his arms on the patio, and she could see that the curls of blond hair on his tanned chest were slicked dark with sweat and cold water from the hosepipe he must have used to wash with.

She had always thought of herself as a town girl. Not glamorous or super slick, but definitely an urban dweller.

But the sight of Max as he towelled himself off in the sunshine hit her hard in what was most definitely a more primitive part of her brain.

There was a reason why the race of cavemen had survived—and this was it.

From where she was standing she could see the muscles working all down his back and shoulders as he washed away the last remaining brown flakes.

One thing was for sure.

Max Treveleyn was not hot chocolate fondue at all.

Max Treveleyn was a huge tower of freshly baked choux pastry profiteroles filled with whipped vanilla-scented Chantilly cream and then smothered in warm, molten bitter chocolate sauce. So that each bite gave a smooth tang of dark chocolate on the outside but was creamy and luscious in the middle, squidging out of the sides of your mouth if you tried to eat a whole one all at once.

How could she have got it so badly wrong?

Because if there was one dessert that she could not resist it was chocolate profiteroles.

A shiver of anticipation swept through Daisy as she considered how long it would take her to dash to her car with her wet dress and pretend that she hadn't changed her mind. It would only take a few minutes, and she could drive away and put this whole crazy idea down to a near-miss.

There was not an ounce of fat on his back. Each muscle and sinew seemed defined and pumped as he worked. The last time she had seen a body like that was on TV one evening, when she'd been flicking channels and had come across a swimming contest where the male swimmers were explaining the different strokes. Topless. Wearing small trunks.

That had been on film. Seeing it for real only a few yards away was quite a different matter. Max was not a professional dancer, or an athlete in any way, but if he ever wanted a change in direction he could be. She would even write the recommendation herself.

Were men *born* with shoulders like that?

At least Max was wearing pants.

As she watched, dry-mouthed, it was a guilty pleasure simply to take a moment to watch as his biceps and the muscles in his back and shoulders moved as he swept the bucket of water up and tipped it over his long blond hair.

He really was spellbinding.

She was ogling the man she was going to be working with over the next few days.

Oh, boy.

Why, oh, why did she always have to lust after the handsome ones who were so far out of her league as to be on another planet? She had been here before. Okay, a chocolate shop in Paris was not exactly the same as a country garden in deepest English countryside, but it was just the same. One look. One smile. And she was right back to being a girl from nowhere who was putty in the hands of a powerful gorgeous man.

In other words—she was pathetic.

She had learnt from her mistake with Pascal and knew precisely what she had to do. Accept the fact that she was attracted to this man and get on with her work. No touching. Simple.

She would handle this her usual way. By keeping him distant. That was the thing.

Max was going to help her take a step closer to opening her own chocolate shop and making the dream she had shared with her precious father come true. He had sacrificed so much for her—she owed it to her dad as well as to herself to give this contest everything she had.

If she was really lucky Max would keep his top on.

And if he didn't?

Just at that moment he whipped a towel from the back of a garden chair and turned around. And looked at her.

Really looked at her.

As though he was seeing her for the first time and he liked what he saw. His eyes met hers, and for the first time in her life Daisy knew beyond any doubt what it felt like to be the object of a man's total admiration and respect. Her heart and her mind sang.

The smile lines at the sides of his mouth lifted up and he nodded. But his eyes never left hers.

'Nice outfit,' he commented. 'It looks a lot better on you than me.'

'Undoubtedly true, but thank you all the same. I'm considering giving your chocolate another chance—but first there is something you need to know.'

He gave her a lazy smile and wrapped the towel around his shoulders before stretching both arms onto the back of the chair. 'Go ahead. I'm all yours.'

Daisy paused for a moment, then lifted her chin, heart thumping. 'Okay. Short version,' she replied. 'You already know that my dad was a baker, but he loved chocolate. People used to come for miles to order special chocolate birthday cakes, and even a couple of chocolate wedding cakes—but they were not so popular back then as they are now.'

Her hands stilled and she lowered the bowl holding her wet dress onto the patio.

'But he was never satisfied with the block chocolate he bought from the local wholesaler. So every week there would be deliveries arriving in the post from suppliers with strange foreign names. From South America, Africa, Belgium.' She looked up at Max and nodded. 'I had the best stamp collection in my school, and for a while I thought Flynn's bakery was going to become Flynn's Bakery and Chocolate Shop.'

As Max watched, her throat seemed to tighten, and she turned away from him and licked her lips.

'But somehow it didn't happen. When I asked him about it, he said that business had fallen away and we didn't have the money to invest in more chocolate work. He was a single dad doing the best he could. He'd come back to it later.' Daisy coughed and shook her head. 'He died of cancer three years ago, and I found the recipe I showed you earlier tucked into the back of a chocolate recipe book. He had been working on the perfect mixture for his own brand of chocolate for years and never told me.'

Max took a breath, as though he was about to offer his condolences, but stayed silent, letting her talk, letting her tell him in her own way.

She reached into her overall pocket and pulled out the precious piece of paper she had rescued from Delores. She turned around to face Max. 'So you see, this is not just about the contest. This is personal. I want to honour his memory in the best way I can, and this is the way I can do it. That means that you are going to have to prove to me that I can trust you. Because you will not be given a third chance. Not with me.' Daisy smiled and blew out hard. 'And now I have become stupidly sentimental. And very bossy. Crazy, huh?'

She lifted her hand to wipe away a tear from her cheek, and gasped as the paper fluttered to the patio stones.

Instantly Max swept down to pick it up, but as he stood up and presented it to Daisy she looked up into a face so full of sadness and regret and longing and understanding that her own heart took a second beat. Because at that second she felt a bond with this man she'd only known for a few hours which was so deep and so powerful that it made her dizzy.

Daisy was lost in those hypnotic blue eyes, wiping away sensible thought and replacing it with an unbidden desire to connect with this remarkable man.

This was probably why, without his asking permission or forgiveness, she allowed him to wipe away the single tear that had fallen onto her cheek with his thumb.

'I am so sorry for your loss. I truly am. Thank you for telling me. And for giving me a second chance to show you that I can make this work. For you, me and your dad,' he said seriously.

'In that case,' she replied with a small sniff,

'if we are going to make some more chocolate this afternoon we had better start on the cleaning. So… Where do you keep your mop?'

CHAPTER SIX

'WELL, that took a lot longer than I expected.' Daisy sighed as she ducked her head to step down into the kitchen. 'Your kitchen is so wonderfully cool. It's bliss.'

'Thanks. I'm glad that you like it,' Max replied as he flung an arm out towards the kitchen table and chairs. 'How about some coffee to keep us going? Hopefully we won't have to spend another two hours cleaning after the next batch.'

'Please. And don't even joke about that.' Daisy coughed and waved her arm around as dust flew up from every surface. 'I…er…take it you haven't been to the cottage for a while?'

'I spent three weeks over the Christmas holiday here with Freya. Kate had booked a ski holiday with her new boyfriend,' Max replied, then paused before shrugging. 'Who is now her new fiancé, by the way, so it was down to me.' He half turned towards Daisy as he filled the kettle and smiled. 'Do you remember what the weather was like in January? The snow fell for five days without a break. It was the first time in years that the village was cut off—and you know what? It was wonderful. I would not have missed it for the world.'

'Wonderful?' Daisy looked at him in shock. 'How did you manage with a little girl to amuse and take care of?'

'My first stop on day one had been the supermarket, so we had a full refrigerator and store cupboard. We didn't starve. It might sound weird, but even lugging logs to feed the open fires turned into fun when I was pulling them on the same wooden sledge I used as a boy, through snowflakes the size of large coins falling vertically from the sky.'

'You do make it sound rather magical.' Daisy sighed again. 'Your little girl must have adored it.'

'It *was* magical, and Freya loved every second. The village had turned into a winter wonderland, which to a seven-year-old like Freya was like a fairytale come alive. Complete with snowball fights, sledging contests on the gentle hillside behind the house, and a real Christmas tree from the local forest. And you should have seen the snowmen we made.'

Daisy found a clear spot on the table to rest her elbows. 'Freya is a very lucky girl. My January was rather different. You can imagine what a nightmare the snow is when you are being paid to create someone else's wonderful New Year party. I spent every hour of the day working with Tara just to keep up with the orders. Then battling through the weather to make our deliveries. It was madness in the city.'

'Freya and I are both lucky to have avoided that.'

Daisy stopped rummaging around inside her huge shoulder bag and glanced up at him. 'I was admiring the photographs of Freya when I was getting changed. Do you manage to get back to see her very often?'

Max rested his hands on the back of a chair for a second, then lifted them away and raised them shoulder-high as he spoke. 'Often?' he repeated sadly, his eyebrows crunching down as creases formed on his brow. 'As often as I can. But this last Christmas was pretty special.'

Max busied his hands pulling down mugs and plates from the shelves above the work-tops. 'Problem is, these days I spend most of the year in St Lucia so the cottage is left empty. It doesn't like it. And the garden is a jungle.'

He looked up just as Daisy reached over and touched the first of two large hand-painted beakers hanging from hooks below the dresser shelves. He had to stop himself from jumping up and snatching the china from her fingers.

Freya's favourite cup! His little girl would be heartbroken if anything happened to it.

'It's okay. I have some mugs here,' he said quickly. 'Would you prefer coffee or tea?'

'Tea, please—if we have milk. Otherwise coffee would be fine,' Daisy replied, and shuffled into a comfier spot on the padded seat cushion.

'Oh, we have milk. There may even be cheese and crackers. And if we don't want our own cooking tonight we could always have dinner at the local pub. The chef is Italian and some of his regional dishes are pretty good—especially the braised beef and... What?' he asked as she looked blankly at him.

'Dinner?' Daisy looked at Max as though he

had suggested running off to join the circus. 'Why would I want to have dinner here?'

She tilted her head slightly, and there was enough of an edge in her voice to drop the temperature in the room a few degrees lower.

'I think there may have been a misunderstanding. I am driving back to London tonight, with some blocks of Treveleyn Estate chocolate. I hope that you did not expect me to work on the recipes here and travel back and forth to London every day.'

'Oh, no. I would not expect you to do that.' Max raised one eyebrow higher that the other. 'I expected you to stay the night so that we can work on the recipes together here tomorrow. Sugar? Or are you sweet enough?'

Daisy sucked in a breath, because the way his eyes were totally focused on hers was making her dizzy, and the fact that he was holding out a sugar bowl at the same time only served to confuse her more.

'So let me get this straight.' She blinked and waved away the sugar. 'First of all you have dragged me down to this back-of-beyond cottage, which took me ages to find, only to tell me that you expect me to make the chocolate. And now I find out that you expect *me* to stay the night so that I can…'

'Work on the recipes first thing in the morning with fresh chocolate. I thought that it would save you the long drive to London tonight and then back again in the morning,' Max replied with a smile in his voice, and passed her a steaming hot mug of tea.

Daisy broke eye contact and shook her head slowly from side to side, aware that her mouth had fallen open. She closed it with a snap. 'You do know that you are impossible, don't you? Contrary to common belief, not all women are mind-readers.' She waved the fingers of her right hand across her brow. 'Unless someone says the actual words, I have no way of knowing what is going on in that brain of yours. Which leaves me only one question.'

'Please—ask away,' Max replied, lifting his coffee towards her.

'Do you have any other great thoughts that you want to share with me? Because I have no intention of staying the night. And I certainly have not come here to cook the chocolate.'

Daisy glanced around the tiny space around her, which was devoid of anything remotely resembling a worktop or catering equipment.

She was used to pristine shiny stainless steel counters, like the ones at Barone and in Tara's catering unit. Right now the best she was going to find was a wooden butcher's block and this small kitchen table.

The contrast was so enormous it wasn't even funny.

'Do you even have an oven that works? Because it is has taken me a year to collect together all of the specialist chocolatier's equipment I need at Tara's, and I am very picky about where I cook. Very. Picky. I had planned to spend most of tomorrow experimenting with the chocolate in a few standard recipes. In my own kitchen. Using my own equipment.'

She lowered her forearms back to the table, lifted her chin and stared at him down her nose. She could only do that because he had slouched down in his seat and was, for once, lower than she was.

'But to do that I need to have a couple of kilos of this amazing chocolate I have been promised. No chocolate. No cooking. No contest. Am I getting through to you? Max? Because I suggest that we make the chocolate first, before we move onto grandiose plans of what to cook with it.'

In the silence that followed his eyes remained completely focused on the cup of black coffee he was holding, blowing on its surface.

It left plenty of time for her to attune herself to his body, and the way it responded to tiny changes in his movement.

The muscles in his arms below the sleeves of his small, tight T-shirt flexed and twitched in the action, and her poor heart thumped in tune with every beat of the pulse she could see in his neck. The faint breeze coming in through the kitchen window did nothing to dissipate the heat of this broad-shouldered man sitting only inches away, who was still looking at his coffee with those laser blue eyes.

And it annoyed her enormously that she felt a twinge of jealousy that he was not looking at her with that much rapt attention.

The seconds stretched and Daisy breathed in slowly, inhaling a complex blend of man, the floral perfume from the climbing musk roses which cascaded down around the window outside, and the old wood of the cottage. Dust and the scent of fresh-cut grass from his clothes wafted towards her as he shuffled on his seat, tilted his chair back and reached backwards for a small metal tin on the pine wood dresser to his side.

Unfortunately for Daisy that meant his body stretched back. His T-shirt lifted to display more of those tight abs, and the muscles inside his trousers clenched hard to keep him balanced.

That was more than could be said for her heart-rate.

Desperately trying to find something—anything—to distract her, Daisy clutched hold of her tea and took a long sip. And then another.

'Try one of these,' Max finally said, as the front legs of his chair reconnected with the tile floor. 'Make you feel a lot better.'

Not so sure about that, Daisy thought, drinking down even more tea, and then realised that Max was holding out a biscuit tin.

She peered inside and saw two fairycakes in paper cases. There was a crude dollop of icing on the top of each one, and pink and purple sprinkles. So, all in all, just about the last thing she would have expected.

What was this man doing to her? How many more surprises did he have up his sleeve?

Just when she thought she had a grip he did something which whipped the carpet out from under her feet.

She picked up one of the cakes and stared at it for a second, before peeling off the paper and biting into it.

'In case you were wondering, Freya and her schoolfriend decided to have a dolls' house tea party yesterday, just before I took off. So I rustled up some super-quick little cakes before her mother caught me messing up her kitchen. The girls enjoyed them.'

He pointed at the remains of her cake, which was halfway between the table and her mouth.

'They may not be chef quality, but what do you think? I did try to follow the instructions on the packet, but they were rather vague and my lovely daughter was no help at all.'

Think? She was expected to *think*? And judge fairycakes? That he'd made from a packet mix?

Oh, why did he have to make fairycakes for his daughter? That was a totally unfair advantage.

Of course there was no way that he could know that some of her most precious family memories were of when her dad had made fairycakes and mini-scones for dolls' tea parties with her mother. Then her mother had died and there had been just the two of them against the world, but standing in that kitchen licking cake batter from a wooden spoon had somehow made it all better.

There was no way for Max to know that. How could he? They had only just met. He did not know a thing about her life and the bumpy road she had travelled to be sitting at this table. Winning this contest could open up all kinds of doors to achieving her dream—and all he could offer her was a packet fairycake.

What *was* it about him that made it impossible for her to stay grumpy with him? It was so very annoying. Especially when he was giving her his last fairycake.

'Actually, I come from a family of bakers,' she replied. 'So I can honestly say that...'

'Yes?' He winced. 'Go on. I can take it.' He flashed her one of those 'oh-lord-please-do-not-do-that-again-because-my-poor-heart-won't-be-able-to-take-it' smiles that lit up the room and made the air between them in this small room seem even hotter.

'Considering that you made them yesterday, and they have probably been bashed around a little between here and London, your tea party cakes are...not bad. Not bad at all. For a packet mix.'

His reply was a smile filled with such genuine pleasure and delight that she could not help but smile back.

'Really? Thanks.'

'Do you often cook with Freya?' Daisy asked as her fingers carefully folded up the paper case into triangles. 'She must love that you take time out to do that with her.'

Daisy was too busy for a few seconds whisking away cake crumbs to notice that Max had not replied, and she glanced up. Then her hands stilled. Because in that split second she had looked at him his face had twisted into an expression of such pain and regret that she wondered if he was physically in pain. And then his eyebrows and jaw relaxed and the pain was gone, but the temperature of the air between them seemed to have dropped several degrees. She already missed the man who had been enjoying his cake only a few minutes earlier.

'Are you okay?' she asked. 'Headache?'

The fingers of his right hand tapped out a beat on the wooden table. 'Nothing that spending more time with my little girl wouldn't cure. But it's her birthday next week—we'll have a great time.'

Oh, how stupid of her. Max was divorced. And his ex-wife had a boyfriend. No—he had said fiancé earlier. Ouch. Being a single dad was hard enough, without his daughter being presented with a new stepdad. Double ouch. That had to be difficult—especially when Max lived in the Caribbean.

Her foolish heart reminded her of her dad, and how precious their one-to-one time had been when she got back from school and the shop closed for the day.

She only hoped that Freya and Max had that kind of relationship during the short time they spent together.

'I hope she likes her chocolate rabbits.'

'And the rabbit poo. How could I forget that?'

He looked up, and his face relaxed just a little more until it was almost back to normal as he smiled across the table at her.

And in that instant Daisy felt that same tug of connection between them that she had sensed in the restaurant twist tighter and tighter, as though a great wheel was being turned inside her stomach, drawing her closer and closer to Max with an invisible rope which she could not possibly break. The feeling was so intense that when he spoke every other sound in the room and the garden outside seemed to fade away, and his words reverberated inside her chest and head.

'We both have our own reasons for making this chocolate today. So let's give this our best shot. Besides…' He smiled. 'Dolores will be missing us.'

Max stood back from the mixer and stretched his right arm out high above his head, to try and relieve the tension that had been building up over the past few hours.

They had worked so hard—both of them—but Daisy was still not happy with the chocolate.

The good news was that Dolores had decided that she loved them again once Max had managed to find the instruction manual that had been supplied with the mixer. Of course the electrical settings had been written in French, so Daisy had had to translate as best she could, but with much prodding of buttons and exasperated stomping they had finally found the programme that matched what they were trying to achieve. Molten chocolate paste. Smooth, refined and delicious.

The even better news was that Daisy had stayed with him every step of the way, cheering when the paddles started moving the way they should, and standing shoulder to shoulder with him when his digital thermometer gave up and the cocoa liquor looked more like lava than a luxury ingredient. She had never given up or run off screaming.

Rolling his shoulders backwards, Max paused for a second to watch Daisy. She was standing with her stomach resting on the worktop, her body hunched over the tiny sample pots which she sniffed and tasted. Her hands were in constant motion, noting down the subtle differences in each blend they had so carefully prepared.

He was close enough to see the way her red hair curled up at the base of her neck in the heat, and the cute way her lips came together as she concentrated on the sample she was holding in her hand.

He came across to lean one hand on the worktop, inhaling the intoxicating blend of perfumes on her skin. She smelt of everything good in his world. Vanilla. Spice and chocolate. Very good chocolate.

She was really quite remarkable.

'I don't understand it. We have already tried three variations on this formula, and if I add more vanilla the sweet creaminess will mask the spice in the cocoa… What?'

She half turned to look at him; as though she had been talking to herself and forgotten he was there.

This girl needed a break—and there might be something he could do to help.

'Daisy? A suggestion. Why don't we go outside and take in some fresh air for a few minutes? I don't know about you, but my tastebuds are exhausted. It might do us both good to have a quick break away from all these flavourings.'

Daisy looked past Max at the containers where their previous batches were cooling and blinked. 'That is the best idea I have heard for a while. I had forgotten how overwhelming the smell of chocolate can be when you are making up such large quantities.'

She gave him a quick nod and a smile, then her shoulders seemed to slump with tiredness.

'I shall need a local guide to recommend the finest viewpoints,' she continued in a pretend serious voice. 'And a chair would be wonderful.'

Max responded by taking her elbow and guiding her to the garage door. 'I shall be happy to oblige on both counts.' And then he stopped as Daisy came to an abrupt halt. 'Is everything okay?'

'The sun is almost setting. Wow. I had no idea it was this late.'

'Best time of the day. Here. Try this for a viewpoint. And it even has a seat.'

Max pointed to an old wooden bench which Daisy had not even noticed on her mad dash that afternoon from the kitchen to the workshop. It was half hidden in a tiny arc of flowering bushes and potted plants which almost covered the surface of a small paved patio area. Completely secluded and separated from the cottage by a low hedge, it was a perfect private space.

And quiet. So quiet and peaceful that when Max sat down next to her she did not think it bizarre that he was happy to lean back against the carved wood, his legs outstretched, so that they could both sit and enjoy the last warm rays of the sun on their faces before it set below the trees.

A pair of black swifts calling to each other above her head broke the reverie.

'What a lovely spot,' Daisy murmured after a few minutes. 'I can see why you would want to come back here.'

Max closed his eyes and laid his head back against the wooden bench, so that when he spoke it was as though his words were addressed to the sky.

'The first time I saw this garden I was fourteen years old and had just arrived from St Lucia after a nightmare flight. My parents had been killed in a car crash and my grandmother was my designated guardian. It was January. I was angry, bitter, and so cold I thought I was going to freeze to death. Which at the time felt like a far better option than trying to come to terms with the shock of being taken away from everything I knew.'

Daisy stopped breathing so that the sound of her taking a breath would not disturb Max. But he'd opened his eyes and with a shake of his head rocked forward to rest his elbows on his knees.

'Until then my life had been constant heat and living outdoors in tropical forests and wonderful beaches. Long sunny days playing with my friends and making my own fun.' He sighed out loud. 'I didn't want to be here. I felt as though I had been ripped away from my one and only home. And I made sure that everyone around me knew that. Loudly. In every way possible.'

'Oh, Max. How terrible that must have been for you. I am so sorry.'

He turned and smiled at her, but there was enough sadness in Daisy's eyes that the depth of her feeling startled him. Her hand slid over across the bench and she meshed her fingers between his.

She had lost both her parents too, and the power of their mutual understanding hit him so hard that Max swallowed down a lump in his throat that he had not felt for a long time.

'How did you…? I mean, how did you get through that?' Daisy asked.

Max looked around him from side to side. 'Boarding school helped. I was mostly feral, but I had a passion for sports and somehow the teachers kept me indoors long enough to get it through my thick skull that actually science and mathematics were useful things for a cocoa farmer to know about. Because one thing kept me going—my promise to myself that I would go back and work the estate.'

He stared down at their linked hands and waggled his fingers before taking a firmer grasp of hers.

'But that was not the only thing.' He smiled, and with his free hand lifted a long strand of her hair which had fallen onto her brow. 'My grandmother gave me a gardening project of my own to do. Right here. In her secret garden.'

Daisy's eyes widened in understanding, and she looked around her in even greater admiration.

'Did you make all this on your own? It's wonderful. How did you know what to plant?'

His reply was to half turn on the bench. 'Before I answer that question I need you to lie back and close your eyes. Go on—just for a moment. Close your eyes. I'll be right here all the time. Now, you are going to have to at least try and relax. There. That's better. Much better.'

Daisy flashed him one final glance before letting her head fall back. She sighed in delicious contentment as Max slid forward on the bench. Without letting go of her hand.

'Now, don't say anything, but focus on what you can smell. Flowers. Plants. We have spent hours working inside, so feel free to go mad; I know you can do it if you try.'

'Smell? I don't know. I'm a stranger to anything even vaguely horticultural.'

'Nope. I don't believe a word of it. Surprise

yourself. Here. I'll help. Open up your other palm. That's right. What's the first thing that comes into your mind?'

Daisy felt something drop onto the palm of her hand, and was so startled that she almost opened her eyes, but Max stroked the back of her hand with his thumb, calming her.

Her fingertips ran the length of a light dry stem with tiny blossoms at one end.

'This feels like a flower, but there doesn't seem to be any petals,' she replied, then lifted her hand towards her face and inhaled. Instantly an intensely aromatic sweet scent filled her nostrils, and it was so heavenly that Daisy surprised herself by laughing out loud. 'Oh, it's lavender. I love lavender. Oh, that is wonderful. How inspired of you to plant lavender.'

'That was my clever grandmother's idea. She never did like chilli peppers and Caribbean foods. But she knew about plants and how a particular perfume could take you back to a place and a time. We couldn't grow mango or bananas in this garden, but we could grow the kind of flowers that my parents had had in their garden on St Lucia—lavender, musk roses and jasmine. So that is what I planted here. To connect me back to the island.'

With a smile in his voice Max added, 'And to enjoy late on a summer evening when you have been making chocolate for hours. Do you like it?'

Daisy breathed in the warm air and her senses went into overload at the complex combination of perfumes from the flowers which grew in such profusion all around her, the lavender she had crushed between her fingers, and the pervading smell of cocoa on her clothing and hands.

'Oh. Oh, Max. That is…'

'I know. Two different worlds but they come together so perfectly.'

'That was clever. I think we all have places and moments we associate with specific smells—but this is just gorgeous. If only we could find a way of capturing this aroma. *Oh!*'

Daisy's eyes shot open and she opened her mouth to speak, but Max was right there, grinning at her.

In a flash she knew why he had brought her out here.

'I know. And that is what we should do. The cocoa has more than enough spice—we need more perfume, more fragrance. I am thinking English country garden with a West Indian edge. Can you do that? It would be a long way from classical chocolate, but I think it could work.'

'Lavender. Rosewater. Yes. Of course. Fusion cooking is everywhere. That would be totally brilliant,' Daisy squealed, biting down on her bottom lip and clutching at both of Max's hands as he drew her back to her feet. 'I can make a warm chocolate cake that will knock their socks off. With perhaps some lavender and coconut ice cream on the side. Oh, Max. Has anyone told you recently that you are a genius?'

'Not recently.' He nodded. 'But I am prepared to accept the title. Oh, and by the way, thank you, Daisy. Thank you for giving me a second chance.'

Max closed the gap between their bodies, and the expression on his face was so overwhelmingly full of understanding and emotion that the invisible bond that drew her to him tightened so much it was impossible for her to resist.

It seemed only natural for him to tip her chin towards him, slant his head, and press his lips against hers. Softly at first, then firmer, harder, wider.

And Daisy kissed him back, filling her lips and mouth with such luscious sweet warmth that any lingering resistance melted away and she moved deeper into the kiss for a moment longer before she felt Max pull back.

His pupils were dilated, his breath felt hot and fast on her neck, and she could sense his heartbeat racing to match her own.

Daisy pressed the palms of both hands flat against the front of his T-shirt so that she could feel the pace of his heartbeat speed faster as he gently lifted a strand of her hair behind one ear.

'I do have one more suggestion,' he whispered.

'Um…?' Daisy murmured, her eyes scanning his face, focusing on the last rays of sunlight on the white thin scars on his chin and across his eyebrow.

His fingertips slid down from her forehead to her chin in one smooth motion, as though he was frightened to lose contact with her lovely smooth skin, which glowed in the soft, warm light of dusk.

'I would love to make that fusion chocolate tonight, but it's getting late. As in *very* late. Way too late for you to drive safely back to London. So...why *don't* you stay here tonight? Think about it. We could carry on working and make an early start on the recipes in the morning.'

His fingers stilled on her chin, but his eyes were firmly locked onto hers.

'Will you stay here with me tonight, Daisy Flynn?'

CHAPTER SEVEN

'STAY? Spend the night in the cottage with you?'

Daisy froze, her heart racing, as she tried to force air into her lungs and clear her head.

She already told him that wasn't an option… hadn't she?

But that had been before… Oh, boy.

She slowly, gently, pressed her hands against the strong, warm muscles of his chest to try and create some sort of physical distance between them. Because being so close to him, his mouth and his eyes and his body, was too tempting for any girl to stand and try and form logical thought at the same time.

Stay the night? Her fingers warmed to the heat from his body, and just for a second the sensual aroma of Max and the garden threatened to overwhelm her. But she had been here before. She knew that staying overnight would be a big mistake.

'I'm not sure that would be a very good idea, Max,' she said quietly. 'I know that you are concerned, and I thank you, but I have so much to do in London tomorrow. It would be much better if I head back as soon as we've made up the chocolate.'

Instantly the old frown lines appeared on his forehead, and she kicked herself for being the cause of them.

'We are on a remote country lane, without streetlights, and there is no way we can blend this batch in under four hours—even if the perfect combination of flavours jumps out at us first time,' he argued.

He peered at his wristwatch.

'Make that five hours. You could easily get lost and you must be tired,' he added. 'If it makes any difference, search parties and St Bernard dogs are a little hard to find in this neck of the woods.'

His fingertips caressed her jawline, and she almost melted with the pleasure of it.

'I don't want you to get lost. Not. One. Little. Bit.'

Max lowered his head so that they were at

the same eye level, and every ounce of resistance fled.

At that very minute an alarm signal sounded from inside the workshop.

'Dolores!' Daisy gasped, and stepped back as fast as she could, breaking the connection. 'I think your old girl is jealous again.' And with that she lifted her head and staggered back across the patio and through the garage door.

Daisy turned over in the bed and tugged the quilt high up under her chin, but then her toes felt cold and exposed to the cool air. She tried again but the same thing happened, so she gave up and sat back against the headboard, bringing her knees up towards her chest.

She was in the spare bedroom in Max's cottage. In Freya's bed. Totally annoyed with herself and even more annoyed with Max for being so right.

It had been after three before Dolores was finally turned off for the night and their precious, wonderful chocolate was safely collected. By the time Max had guided her towards the kitchen door in the moonlight she had been so tired that she'd hardly been able to keep her eyes open. Getting behind the wheel of a car would not only have been dangerous to anyone else on the roads, it would have been suicidal.

So she'd been forced to admit defeat and accept his offer of a bed for the night—Freya's bed, of course. Worse, Max had insisted that she use the shower first, and in her half-dead state she had practically fallen asleep in there and used most of the hot water.

Perhaps it was guilt that had stopped her from collapsing into a coma the moment her head hit the pillow. Instead she had barely dared to breathe as she lay awake, trying to keep as still and quiet as possible, listening to the sound of Max's footsteps as he pottered around the cottage. The hiss of the shower and the gentle tapping of his bare feet on the kitchen tiles. The sound of his footsteps just down the hall. Only feet away from where she was lying.

If she wanted to, she could slip out of this tight single bed and skip the three steps to the double bed she had spied earlier through the half open door.

Max would not turn her away. She had no

doubt that he needed the comfort and warmth of her touch as much as she needed him.

Daisy closed her eyes and recalled in every sensual detail what it had felt like when he kissed her on the patio. Warmth and controlled strength all wrapped up in a gentle smile and a sweet, sweet mouth.

She propped herself up on one elbow and punched the pillow several times. Then felt guilty about taking out her very personal frustration on an innocent bag of feathers.

She had got herself into this mess—and she had better get herself out of it. Fast.

A door latch fell. Max was out of the bathroom, walking down the hallway, and then he stopped outside her door, probably listening for her snoring or a polite invitation for him to join her in the single bed.

And, oh, that was more tempting than she could admit.

Loneliness did that to people.

Especially when there was a chance that Max Treveleyn might just have the right kind of glue to bring back together the tiny fragments of her broken heart and make it whole again.

If she let him.

But she wouldn't. She couldn't. Because that would mean having to watch him walk away. He could not be here for his own daughter. What chance did *she* have? Every time he took off back to St Lucia it would be like losing him all over again.

Daisy stared at the bedroom door over the edge of the quilt, willing it to open and terrified that it would at the same time.

But it didn't, and his footsteps moved away, back to his own room.

Right decision. For both of them.

Now all she had to do was work with Max for three more days and then she could reclaim her nice, orderly and calm life and focus on the shop. This was what she wanted. Wasn't it?

A huge yawn stretched her face wide. Perhaps she could just catch a few hours' rest before starting back to London?

Max had busied himself with tidying the kitchen and clearing away the last remnants of their quick meal while Daisy was in the shower, but every nerve and sinew of his body had been totally attuned to the tiny sounds coming from the corridor.

It had almost been a relief when he'd finally heard the extractor fan close and the tap-tap of her feet on the floor as she padded the few steps to Freya's bedroom.

It had been torture to work side by side with her on that final miraculous blend of cocoa but he had done it. He'd had to. This was their future. But even their frantic drive to finish the chocolate hadn't been able to overcome the tension in the room, where every physical contact had seemed magnified a thousand times.

At least they had kept their hands and minds fully occupied. But now? Now he had time to work through the turmoil of the events of the day, starting with trying to clear a path through the jungle of a garden and ending up kissing a girl he had only met a few days earlier who had kissed him right back. And meant it.

He had relived those few minutes when he'd held her in his arms so many times over the past hour, and the more he thought about it the more it seemed like a dream, driven by the exhilaration of what they had achieved and the heady atmosphere of dusk on the patio.

Max scrubbed at his hair with a rough hand-towel and sat down on the edge of the bed, his elbows high on his knees. What he wanted to do was stand outside Freya's room again and listen for Daisy to check that she was asleep. But he dared not move because every step he took would be heard in the still and silent old cottage, where every piece of wood creaked and expanded like a living thing.

What had he been thinking?

Or maybe that was the problem—he had not been thinking at all. He had simply given in to those selfish impulses that only led to heart-break and bitter disappointment.

Max rubbed his hands hard over his face, then gave his hair a final tousling before tossing the towel into the laundry basket.

Daisy was a lovely girl and he liked her. He liked her a lot. In fact he liked her more than he should. And a whole lot more than he had any business to.

Max padded across the sanded wooden floor

to the ancient small bedroom window and un-latched the window as quietly as he could.

It was early morning, a couple of hours before dawn, and dew was settling on the roses which grew in tangled profusion on the wooden trellis which ran the full height of the outside wall.

The air was almost as refreshing as the shower water, and he was grateful for the chance to cool his head and selected parts of his body, mostly below the waist, before they compounded the trouble and took him to places he could not walk away from.

Max shook his head.

He was physically exhausted, emotionally drained, and somehow, without meaning to, he had just added a whole new layer of trouble and stress to an already stressed situation.

He had just made the first batch of Treveleyn Estate chocolate. And it was better than he could have hoped for. Daisy had helped to make that possible—and he was grateful. She could have walked out on him several times and he would not have blamed her after Dolores had embarrassed herself—but Daisy had given him a second chance.

Second chances did not come along very often in his life.

Trouble was, you had to know the true cost of that chance before you dived into it head-first. And that was what was going to keep him awake tonight.

Snuggling back down under the quilt, Daisy closed her eyes for a moment and let the tiredness overwhelm her. After what seemed like minutes, she half opened her eyes and watched sunlight creep around the edge of the curtains, sending shadows across the room. Dawn had come early. She lifted up her left arm and peered at her watch.

Then sat bolt upright in bed, which made her so dizzy that she had to lie down again.

Ten a.m.! This was not dawn—it was the middle of the day. She had not slept this late for months. Even if she worked half the night her internal body clock usually clicked in around seven. Winter and summer.

This country life was having a strange effect on her.

For one thing she had broken every rule in

the book and agreed to take a risk on a man and a chocolate that were worlds away from her normal life. She should have left yesterday, when Dolores had given her opinion about that first batch of chocolate. But she had stayed, and in the end Max and Dolores had worked their magic and together they had produced chocolate which she could only hope was as remarkable this morning as it had been when they'd unloaded it from the mixer during the night.

And secondly—well, secondly she did not usually go around kissing divorced men she had just met. That was a first. And the fact that she had enjoyed it enormously did not change the fact that she might just have made a huge mistake. Far from it. If anything it made it worse.

Daisy sighed out loud, flung the cover off and swung her legs over the edge of the bed.

She twiddled her toes for a moment, then shook her head and smiled.

When it came to Max Treveleyn her no-touching policy was not working one little bit.

Her smile faded and she stepped over to the window, drawing back the curtain and looking out over the garden. It looked so different early in the morning. The fine weather had broken during the night and there was a fine drizzle of rain in the air. It should have been dull and grey, to reflect the broken clouds in the sky, but instead the sheen of water on the green bushes and flowers made the colours gleam and shine bright and clean.

In this light it was a completely different place. As though the rain had washed away the past and the garden had started the new day with a clean slate.

If only it was so simple for people…

She should not have kissed Max.

There was never going to be any sort of relationship for them going forward. How could there be? He would be going back to St Lucia after his daughter's birthday party and that would be the end of their work together. Even if they won the contest she would be based in Cornwall while he shipped cocoa from his estate thousands of miles away.

He had never mentioned having a girlfriend back on the island, and it was not a conversation she was going to start any time soon, but somehow she knew that he was not the kind of man who would have a girl in every port.

So where did that leave her?

Simple. It left her with three more days of working side by side with Max—including two nights in a lovely romantic hotel in Cornwall.

But they had kissed. And they had both meant it.

The cold chill of having been to this place before sent a shiver across her shoulders even in the warm bedroom.

Pascal Barone had promised her the world. A brilliant future and a wonderful life together. But in the end he had let her down just when she'd needed him most.

Max was not Pascal—far from it. But she had trusted her heart and her instincts to keep her safe before, and they had betrayed her by being too open and too welcoming. She had needed love in her life after her father had died, and she needed it now. Deny it as best she could, that moment last night when Max had pressed his lips to hers…her poor parched heart had soaked in every precious second of that glorious intimacy and physical sensation like a desert in the rain.

It frightened her just how much she needed someone like Max in her life.

She wanted to be intimate with someone she could call her friend as well as her lover. And here was Max. Offering her...what? A few days of fun before he took off? Leaving them both with broken hearts and regrets?

She had never had a one-night stand in her life, and this was not the best time to start.

No. It would be better if she left now. Said goodbye and thanks for the choc, and see you in Cornwall. Put the whole thing behind them and get back to being professional colleagues who were attending a conference together.

She could do that.

Yeah, right. *And the garden was suddenly full of a squadron of purple piglets in pink tutus, singing as they flew across the sky.*

Daisy pushed herself away from the window. Time to get dressed and talk to Max.

She strolled into the kitchen and her senses were instantly struck with the most amazing perfume coming from a vase of flowers on the wooden table.

A crystal water jug had been filled to over-flowing with white roses, jasmine, lavender and honeysuckle—in fact all of the stunning fragrant flowers that she had enjoyed in the secret garden at dusk.

There was no formal arrangement—but these flowers did not need one. They were glorious. A still life made real by the man who had planted and grown these blossoms and loved them because they reminded him of happier times.

Well, she knew about that. And it linked her to him even more than she could say. Without having to say the words she knew that from now on, whenever she smelt those floral scents, it would take her back to this cottage and this garden and the man who had kissed her at dusk in the secret garden he had created.

It was no good. She could not resist reaching out with one hand and lifting one of the musk roses to her nose by its stem. Instantly she dropped it, and sucked on her finger where it had pricked her.

'Good morning,' came a familiar voice from

the door to the garden, and Daisy looked up just as Max strolled in, his hands full of supermarket carrier bags.

Her poor treacherous heart jumped onto a trapeze and performed some very impressive gymnastics just at the sight of him.

Max stood in the doorway, framed by the thick wooden beams above his head and the bright sunlit garden behind him, so that his face was in shadow, and in that single dizzy moment Daisy felt as though her life was spinning on a pinhead.

She could stay and hope that this fire inside her would light the beacon for a long-standing loving relationship—but that fire would be fuelled by her dreams of her own chocolate shop. Because one thing was for sure. Max had no intention of leaving his cocoa plantation. Not even for his own child.

Or she could go and start all over again. And one day she might be in a position to buy his cocoa as a customer. Safe and secure and working for herself, on a path she had chosen. And probably never see him again.

She had promised herself that she would never

make the compromise her father had made—
and yet here it was. Staring her in the face.

But either way she could not—*would* not—
let him know how she felt. Simply standing in
his kitchen watching him shuffle from foot to
foot, pretending that nothing had happened, was
awkward enough.

*Time to get back in control. And to get as far
away from Max as possible.*

'And good morning to you too.' She gulped.
'I see that you have been up early, scavenging
for supplies, while I caught up with my sleep.
Here. Let me help.'

Max dropped the bags onto the table, his attention totally focused on the contents. 'Seeing
as dinner last evening consisted of ham and
cheese sandwiches and fizzy drinks, I thought
that the least I could do was to provide a decent
breakfast. I'm not used to having a professional
chef in the house, so a trip to the local supermarket was in order.'

He dived into the bags and brought out
each item for her inspection as though it was
buried treasure. 'We have everything we need
for a cooked breakfast, plus mushrooms and

extra ham. Fresh bread, butter, lots of jam and marmalade, and a packet of croissants.'

Max sucked in a breath through his teeth as he inspected the croissants, but all the time he had not once looked at her.

'I have never actually been to Paris myself, so I have nothing to compare them against, but...'

'Max.' Daisy reached out and pressed her right hand on top of his to still his frantic motion.

For the first time that morning Max lifted his chin, so that she could see his face in sunlight instead of shadow.

Although his mouth was turned into a gentle half-smile there was a deep crease between his eyebrows, and as she looked closer the deep shadows under his eyes told her that he had probably had less sleep than she had. Those stunning hypnotic blue eyes scanned her face over and over again, as though he was looking for a sign of how she was feeling about him.

They looked at each other in silence for what seemed like minutes.

Then both of them started talking at the same time.

'Ladies first,' Max said, breaking the

crackling electric current that was in the air between them.

'Okay,' Daisy replied. 'The food looks fine, but please stop. It's okay. Just sit down and talk to me.' She released his hand and started undoing the plastic wrap on the croissants before asking, 'Did you get much sleep this morning?'

Max looked at her, then pulled out a chair and started to pull his croissant apart. 'A few hours. Daisy…? About last night. I owe you an apology. I shouldn't have kissed you and I'm sorry that it has put us into an awkward situation.'

Daisy took a deep breath and looked into his face. His last few words had come gushing out in one long rush, and she knew how hard they must have been to say. 'You don't owe me an apology,' she replied simply.

Max shook his head and continued shredding his croissant. 'I think I do. We had both worked hard, it was a lovely evening, and I got caught up in the moment.' He lifted both hands from the table. 'It certainly wasn't planned, but I don't want you to go away today with the wrong idea. I am so sorry, Daisy, but long-distance relationships don't work and affairs are painful. So that only leaves one question.'

Max looked up at her, and this time his face was pale and serious, and each and every one of his frown lines was frozen into sharp relief.

'I'll understand it if you want to hit me over the head with the bacon, but can you forgive my over-active libido and tolerate me enough to work with me as a colleague over the next few days? Because that's all I can offer you. Tell me, Daisy? Is that enough?'

Daisy stared at Max for long enough to see beads of perspiration on his forehead.

It was probably only minutes, but in the silence of the kitchen all she had to listen to was the background soundtrack of birdsong and the thumping of her heart.

Because Max had just told her in his own way that he felt just as much for her as she was feeling for him. And he was trying to create some distance between them to protect them both from the pain of a doomed love affair.

He clearly had no idea that she could see it in his face. And that if anything his words only served to bind them more closely together instead of driving them apart. He was doing this for her as much as himself.

Daisy pushed up from the table and found plates and cutlery, aware that Max was still watching her every move.

Time to put him out of his misery. If he could make the sacrifice and be noble then so could she—by telling him the truth. But not necessarily all of the truth.

'The short answer to your question is yes. It *is* enough.'

She sat back down and reached for butter and jam.

'But there is also a longer answer. Do you remember that Marco mentioned that I had worked for Barone in Paris? Yes? Well, you should know that I met my first love in Paris. He was a chocolatier, and between us we planned to take the chocolate world by storm. We were the best in the business and nothing was going to stop us going right to the top.'

Daisy nibbled on a fragment of her croissant and rubbed the pastry flakes from her fingers as Max listened in silence, his face still intense but more with interest than concern.

'The relationship ended badly, and it has taken me three years of hard work to rebuild my life and my confidence in my abilities to the point where I can even think of going out on my own.'

She put down her knife and leant across the table towards him.

'That's why I want my own shop, where I can make my own decisions. And this contest with your cocoa could help me get there. But if we are going to do this we need to give it everything we have got and not let our personal lives get in the way. Can you do that, Max? Is that enough for *you*?'

Max nodded once, then stretched out his left hand and placed it on her arm, stilling her hand. 'You have my word. I will do whatever I can to help us win this contest. We are a team now. Then we can move forward with our lives. Please believe me—I know how important this conference is for both of us. I can focus on business when I need to.'

'I do believe you. In fact I believe you enough to take your chocolate back to London and do whatever I can to create something amazing for the contest. I will do my best, Max; you have *my* word on that.'

'In that case,' he replied with a small bow, 'would you mind if I gave these croissants to the birds and toasted some crumpets? I am in the mood for something crisp, English and very buttery.'

She locked eyes with him and gave him a small smile that screamed out that she understood perfectly well that he was not simply referring to the food.

'I thought you would never ask.'

CHAPTER EIGHT

MAX straightened his tie with one hand while tugging at the tight button-down collar of his smart business shirt with the other. He had forgotten how restricting formal wear was, but it was worth it—no, Daisy was worth it.

The past two days had been such a whirlwind of activity that it hardly seemed possible that they were actually here, at the hotel in Cornwall, with everything they needed to make Team Treveleyn a total winner. He had lined up buyers for his cocoa beans, Daisy had finalised her recipes, and all they had to do now was work harder than they had ever worked before and pull this off.

Now if only he could remember how to fasten a tie… Perhaps Daisy could help? She was just down the corridor and… Max dropped his hands onto the hotel room desk and stared at his reflection in the mirror.

What was he doing?

The other delegates might be wearing ties, but it was certainly not his style. He hated ties and everything associated with them. He might wear one for the formal presentation he was giving as part of the conference programme. But for a drinks party?

He ripped away the tie and flung it onto the bed, then sighed in relief as he released the top two buttons on his shirt.

So what if he wanted Daisy to see him in a suit for the first time? He didn't want to let her down by turning up to the official welcome cocktail party wearing a Calypso T-shirt, board shorts and flip-flops. She had challenged him to do his best for her and that was precisely what he intended to do.

The suit was part of the professional image he wanted to create for the other delegates and cocoa-buyers—nothing to do with Daisy at all. He had to think of this conference as a business meeting. This was work. Not a holiday with a girl he wanted in his life so badly that it hurt. He knew that he could not and would not have her.

This was not a date, and certainly not a romantic dinner with Daisy.

They had spent most of the long drive from London to Cornwall talking through ideas for his presentation on West Indian cocoa and chatting about chocolate. Talking and talking about anything and everything except the one thing that had made six hours in a small car more than just uncomfortable.

Their kiss. The way his body reacted whenever she was within touching distance and the fact that he'd almost bounced off his seat when her bare arm had brushed against his when he was loading her luggage. The fact that just a whiff of the light floral perfume she wore had seemed to flood his senses every time she'd shuffled in the passenger seat and made driving in a straight line on the left side of the road even more difficult than normal.

And then there was the way her neck had turned red when he'd happened to glance over in her direction when they were stuck in a traffic jam. Funny how there had always seemed to be something fascinating outside her window when that happened, so that she wouldn't have to look him in the eyes.

He shook his head slowly from side to side and shrugged at his reflection.

Who were they both trying to kid?

The attraction between them was powerful and elemental and unlike anything he had felt before. Trying to pretend that it was not happening was only making it worse.

Max ran his hand over his chin. Tomorrow Daisy would be cooking, he would be talking to potential customers and presenting, and they would probably spend so little time together that the conference gala dinner and the announcement of the contest winners would be over before they knew it.

Then it would be back to their lives. One way or another.

One day.

All he had to do was to keep his promise and focus on the business for twenty-four hours. Daisy needed this to move forward in her life. Without him messing that life up for her.

Right. Max rolled his shoulders back. Time to find Daisy.

* * *

A few minutes later he strolled, back straight, into the brightly lit reception room of the hotel, where clusters of guests and conference-goers were chatting around a grand piano. A pianist in evening dress was entertaining the guests with show tunes and light classical pieces.

He quickly scanned the crush around the cocktail bar for Daisy, then frowned. She was not in her room, and from what he could see she wasn't holding court at the bar either. So she was either outside—or in the kitchen.

It seemed to take for ever for him to wind his way across the room, responding to the friendly greetings from other cocoa producers and organic food manufacturers, and he was almost at the entrance to the kitchens when the kitchen doors opened and he caught a flash of a distinctive and unmistakable red-headed girl.

Daisy Flynn *was* in the kitchen. His mouth twisted with concern and annoyance.

After all the hard work she had put into this contest Daisy deserved to be out here, enjoying the piano and mingling with the other guests, not tucked away in the background as though she was unworthy to be with the conference delegates.

She had told him that she was shy and preferred to stay out of the limelight, but this was ridiculous. Maybe it was time for him to make her see that.

He slipped through the doors, pushed both hands deep into the pockets of his suit pants— and simply watched in wonder.

Daisy was standing at the serving hatch, chatting away to the chefs and waiters who were plating the cold first course of the dinner service on the other side of the barrier. Her laughter blended with theirs as the sumptuous-looking arrangement of ingredients was layered onto each plate, ready for the final touches before being served.

The food looked and smelled amazing, but it was Daisy who took his breath away.

He stepped closer, dodging waiters and kitchen staff, to see what she was doing. Daisy had a tiny cone of what looked like paper in one hand and was drizzling molten dark chocolate from its end onto a serving plate to create beautiful patterns of flowers and leaves. It looked to him as though she was writing on the plates with a narrow stream of chocolate. It really was amazingly skilful work, and from the look of it she had been helping out for quite some time. Four or five plates were already done, and on the other side of the table the hotel's pastry chef was plating beautiful mini-cakes and bite-sized chocolate slices onto the decorated plates to be served as dessert for the guests.

As Max walked up to Daisy the pastry chef lifted his chin and said something to her in French that Max did not quite pick up. She shook her head from side to side and carried on until the plate was completely finished. Only then did she squeeze out the tiny amount of chocolate left in the tube onto her little finger and pop it into her mouth. Seconds later her face cracked into a wide grin and she laughed across at the chef, who gave her a short bow from the waist before waving her away, fluttering both hands and kissing the air between them in a gabble of quick French. She giggled in a girlish way that Max had never heard before, and kissed the air coquettishly in return, with a grin.

A wave of ridiculous jealousy swept over Max, which he concealed by pretending to cough.

'Almond liqueur with a touch of real vanilla. Quite delicious, and I am going to steal it at every opportunity,' she said.

And all the while she was laughing, as though she did not have a care in the world, her back to him, oblivious to the fact that he was watching her. Observing every movement of her body.

The way the bracelet around her right wrist sparkled in the kitchen downlights. The way she had brushed back her shiny auburn hair so that it accentuated her long slender neck and creamy smooth skin. The back of her neck held a shower of golden freckles, like cinnamon on the cream of a cappuccino coffee. Just waiting to be licked off and savoured as a special treat.

And where had she found that dress? The sleeveless bodice was in emerald-green covered with black lace which fitted around her upper body and narrowed at her slim waist before flaring out into a floaty black skirt made for dancing. A short skirt. A skirt which only a girl with amazingly long, toned legs and shapely ankles could hope to get away with.

It was perfect for Daisy. *She* was perfect. Just looking at her filled him with such delight that his lips turned up into a smile. It had been worth the long drive in heavy traffic from his cottage to Cornwall just to see Daisy Flynn in a green and black dress jiggling along in a restaurant kitchen.

This was an image he was going to keep with him for the long, lonely nights back on the island.

Just as he was about to say something the kitchen door swung closed behind him, and Daisy half turned towards Max to see who had come in. He opened his mouth to say hello, good evening—something—anything—but he stalled, totally stunned by this lovely woman he could not drag his eyes away from.

She was wearing a touch of simple make up which highlighted her green eyes and sensuously warm copper pink lips, but Daisy did not need it. Her light came from within. The joy inside her shone out as though there was a spotlight under her skin, infusing every cell with radiance and beauty.

She looked stunning. Magical. And so very, very beautiful.

This was not the Daisy he had met only a few days earlier at a food festival stall.

This was the real Daisy, who hid herself underneath a chef's coat and checked trousers. This was the beautiful, funny and talented woman who had somehow got under the barbed wire barrier he had built around his heart and planted herself neatly in the place marked *love*.

The fact that he had not realised that until this moment hit him so hard that he could only stand there like an idiot and stare even harder at Daisy, who was now dancing her way towards him.

Max stopped breathing. No. He could *not* be falling for her.

Attracted, yes—of course he was attracted. Any man with a pulse would be attracted to a lovely woman like Daisy.

Then she gave him a lop sided grin and the pathetic argument about having only met her a few days ago went up in flames and blew him a disbelieving raspberry. He had never expected to feel this way about another woman after Kate.

The girl he had fallen for at first sight.

It couldn't happen twice…could it? He had never expected to fall for Kate and had fallen fast and deep. Now he was in grave danger of doing exactly the same thing again.

And ruining Daisy's life in the process.

He *was* falling for her. Not a country baker's daughter but a uniquely talented woman whom he had never, ever expected to meet in this world. Chocolate had brought them together—but he knew as she grinned back at his no doubt gormless expression that he was going to have to work hard to make sure chocolate kept them apart.

Daisy's dream was to open her own chocolate shop. He could help her to do that by being Max the cocoa-grower. Max the boyfriend and lover would only take her further away from that goal into a life of bitter disappointment and regret.

He was not going to let that happen. Even if it meant burying his feelings deep inside him and holding them there. Out of sight. For her sake.

But that didn't mean that he couldn't drag her

out of the kitchen and help her enjoy herself for at least one evening before they went their separate ways.

'You made it,' she said, with just enough amazement in her voice for his poor brain to pick up that she might actually be pleased to see him. 'And just in time.'

'I'm so sorry, lovely lady,' he teased, and peered over Daisy's shoulder into the kitchen. 'I am looking for one Daisy Flynn. Chef extraordinaire. Usually wearing black and white check trousers and a white top. Have you seen anyone like that around here? Because we're on a tight schedule and I would hate to be late.'

The muscle stopped twitching at the side of his mouth as she sighed in exasperation and rolled her eyes.

'Apologies for being so late,' he said. 'I lost all track of the time.' Then he paused, stepped back, and stared at her appraisingly. 'You look lovely; you should definitely wear a dress more often—especially with those legs.' And he waggled his eyebrows up and down several times.

'Well, I do have a spare set of black and white trousers if you'd prefer me to cover them up?

No?' Daisy replied, covering up her blushes of embarrassment. 'You don't look too bad your-self, actually. That suit fits you perfectly and I suspect you know that. It must be hard, being so naturally tanned and handsome.'

Max lifted his right hand and pressed it against his heart. 'You think I'm handsome?' he asked lightly. 'In that case, madam, my eve-ning is complete. Shall we join the others? Let the schmoozing begin?'

'By all means,' she replied, grabbing her bag. 'Oh—how did your meeting go? Did you come away with an order?'

'Might have. He's gone away to think about it until after the competition tomorrow, but he could be a useful contact. Small order now and then building up as his chocolate business ex-pands. We've arranged to meet tomorrow eve-ning. After we've celebrated winning, of course. That has to come first.'

'Oh, no pressure, then. Okay. Let's do this.' She took a long breath, then slowly exhaled. 'Teamwork, remember? You smooth-talk the room while I listen and smile and talk about cooking to the other chefs. And I stay glued to your side the whole night. Teamwork. Deal?'

'Deal. Get ready to have a great time. This is going to be quite a night.'

Daisy smiled up into his face, and his poor heart jumped so much in a rush of exhilaration and something else far more fundamental that he thanked heaven the sensible part of his brain kicked in before he did something reckless—like slide his hands somewhere, which would not be a good idea in public.

Then his heart opened and every bit of love and joy and affection he felt for this wonderful girl, who seemed totally unaware of just how talented and gorgeous she was, seemed to burst through in a bright bubble of happiness. He almost felt—no, he *knew* he felt happy. After so many years the feeling was almost overpowering.

Forget the contest. Forget the plantation. Tonight was going to be simply about being with Daisy and sharing a magical evening together in this lovely place.

He wanted her as much as he needed her.

Tomorrow would take care of itself. Tonight

he was going to live in the moment and enjoy the company of this stunning woman on his arm.

'I have an idea. Let's go and enjoy ourselves and forget about the contest for a while. We have food—looking good, guys,' he said, tipping two fingers towards the head chef, who grunted back at him and got back to his plates. 'They'll probably force us to drink delicious chilled sparkling wine. It will be tough—but, hey, we're professionals. I think we can cope.'

'Oh, I'm sure we can,' she agreed.

'I think it's time to leave these chefs to their work.' He gestured with his head towards the reception room, where the noise of the guests was growing louder by the second. 'They'll never get those meals out if you hang around in that dress.'

And with that he turned to the door and pushed out his right elbow for her to take. 'Ready to face the music?'

'And dance?' she asked with a lilt in her voice as she hooked her hand through his arm.

'Now, that would be pushing it. My feet? Your toes? Dodgy.'

She glanced down at their feet and wiggled her toes inside her sandals. 'Good point. I do have to dash from one side of a kitchen to the other for several hours tomorrow without blisters, bruising or broken bones. Maybe tomorrow evening?'

'In that case...' Max pushed open the kitchen door and a wall of music, chatter and loud laughter from way too many people crammed into one room hit them like a physical barrier.

'On the other hand we could slip out of the kitchen door and make a run for it,' she whimpered.

'Not going to happen.' He gazed into the room. 'I can see three other cocoa-growers, and most of the organising committee. Let's go and talk all things chocolate on the terrace. You know that you want to.'

With a final wave to the chefs Daisy strolled past Max, who held open the door, and moved along the edge of the crowded room until she came to the long patio doors which led onto the terrace.

And then she stopped dead, frozen to the spot.

Because the man strolling in through those

patio doors as though he owned the hotel was Pascal Barone.

He was still as handsome as ever, and for just one fraction of a second her poor wounded heart expanded and threatened to overwhelm her.

Until she heard Pascal's condescending and arrogant voice.

She had cared about this man once, but now he sounded so grating and so full of self-importance that the hard truth of who he was and how far she had come from being a green young girl on her first trip to Paris hit her—and hit her hard.

Looking at Pascal now, for the first time in three years, she saw him through new eyes. Attractive, elegant, self-confident—and as slick as a slick thing from slick land.

Just then Pascal half turned and looked at her—then looked at her again.

A half-smile, brimming with condescension, creased his clean-shaven olive-skinned face, and he had just opened his mouth to speak when a firm hand gripped Daisy's elbow and propelled her forward until she was within touching distance of Pascal—who, to his credit, appeared just as startled as she felt.

'Mr Barone,' Max said coolly, and he gave Pascal a handshake so firm that the Frenchman winced and flexed his fingers the moment they were released from Max's vice-like grip. 'Max Treveleyn of the Treveleyn Estate, St Lucia. Lovely to meet you.' Max wrapped his arm around Daisy's waist and smiled warmly at her. 'Have you met my lovely chocolate master Daisy Flynn? I consider myself very lucky to have a star like Daisy on my team. She's come up with some stunning ways to present my cocoa.'

As he raised a champagne flute to his lips Pascal's response was to tip the glass ever so slightly towards her in a silent salute and raise one eyebrow.

'Mr Treveleyn. Miss Flynn and I have already met.'

'Well…' Daisy said, trying not to choke, and gave Pascal a short nod. 'This is quite a surprise, Pascal. I didn't think that you were interested in organic chocolate. How is life in Paris these days?'

Pascal smirked, and one side of his mouth lifted dismissively. 'Life in Paris is just fine, thank you. And how is life in...' He lifted his eyebrows, looked upwards and pretended not to remember the name of the small town she came from. 'I'm sorry. The name has completely slipped my mind.'

'Oh, I'm based in London now.' Daisy smiled back through gritted teeth, aware of other guests clustering around the patio doors and strolling out onto the terrace on each side of her. 'Still working as hard as ever.'

Pascal shuffled one step closer. 'I hear you have been working on a range of moulded novelty chocolate body parts. The catering business must be such interesting work.'

Daisy fought down a cutting response to his snide remark, and Max stepped in before she said something which would get them both thrown out of the contest.

'Oh, wonderful work—and innovative. It took a while for me to persuade her to join my team, but the Treveleyn Estate could not wish for a better chocolatier. Daisy is going to knock the socks off those judges tomorrow. You wait and see.'

Pascal nodded with a derisive snort. 'It's good to hear that you are so confident about your chances, Mr Treveleyn. My own team have been working full-time for months to find the most delectable recipes using the finest organic cocoa. I think the judges are going to be quite impressed with what Team Barone come up with.'

Daisy could almost hear the cogs in her brain clanking over as the impact of what Pascal was saying hit home.

'Why on earth would *you* want to take part in this contest, Pascal?' she asked, her mind reeling. 'I thought you were content with your chain of chocolate shops?'

'You know I cannot resist a challenge, Daisy. I have plans to expand into the restaurant trade, and this is a useful opportunity to try out some of our new range of organic chocolate desserts. So, yes, this contest is turning out to be very interesting indeed.' He raised his glass to his lips and glowered at her over the rim.

'The very best of luck to you, Mr Barone.

Now, if you will excuse us, I promised Daisy a glass of champagne to celebrate our new partnership. Have a great evening,' Max said.

'Oh, I will—I certainly will,' Pascal replied with a nasty glint in his eye, and tipped his head to them before turning away to join another group who were probably more useful to his career.

'I think the terrace is calling us. I'll be right back,' Max whispered into her ear, then slipped his arm away and headed out to the bar.

CHAPTER NINE

ON THE terrace, tables had been set with beautiful linens and stained glass lanterns which shed a warm glow in the fading sunlight. A wonderful sweet scent pervaded the patio from the white gardenia plants in full flower, which bloomed in stunning terracotta planters, but the setting was completely lost on Daisy as she tottered away from Pascal with as much dignity as she could on the borrowed heels that Tara had supplied to go with her borrowed dress.

She collapsed down on one of the luxuriously appointed sofas and looked out over the stunning stone terrace, where elegantly dressed men and women were chatting.

The jewels on the women glittered, and fairylights hung from the trees. Everything shone bright and sparkly and new and exciting, and laughter echoed out of the patio doors.

While she felt like a tired old doormat some-one had just wiped their feet on.

The happiness and the excitement of being here had been trampled on and ruined by the blast from her past that was Pascal Barone—and she hated it. Hated the effect he still had on her. Hated that just seeing him again had brought back all of those old feelings of being so inadequate and unworthy and so totally, to-tally inept and useless.

Here she was, surrounded by beautiful peo-ple in a beautiful place, about to eat beautiful food prepared by experts. And she had never felt more worthless.

What had ever given her the idea that she could compete against pros like Pascal? She was a complete phoney. Just another wannabe country bumpkin with self delusions that she could pull this confidence trick off.

'Are you okay?' Max sat down on the sofa next to her and looked into her face as he pre-sented her with a champagne flute. 'I am so sorry. I had no idea that Barone had decided to enter the cooking contest. That was where you trained, wasn't it? But you can relax. The worst part is over now.'

'You have nothing to be sorry for, Max,' Daisy answered, her eyes firmly fixed on the glass of champagne as though mesmerised by the bubbles. 'This is my problem and I have to deal with it. Thanks for getting me out of there. Pascal was…is…'

She swallowed down a long sip while Max joined the dots.

'Pascal. Right. Tell me to get lost if you want, but the chocolatier who let you down in Paris… it was Pascal Barone. Wasn't it?'

Daisy took another long sip of champagne before pushing her chin out and trying with all her might to sound positive when she replied. The last thing she wanted was for Max to realise what an idiot he had chosen to work with.

'Oh, that was years ago. Water under the bridge.' She took another sip, but her hand was shaking so much that she almost dropped the flute and quickly lowered it to the table.

'So I see. Do you want to tell me about it?'

His long, strong and clever fingers were wrapped around hers now, and there was so much genuine sincerity in his voice that his few simple words broke through her barriers.

'No. Yes. Maybe. Oh, this is so embarrassing.'

'Embarrassing or not,' Max replied, stroking the back of her hand with his thumb, 'you are going to have to cook tomorrow knowing the Barone team is in the contest. I think you had better tell me everything. We have a lot riding on this.'

Daisy sighed, low and slow. 'I know. And you're right. But I just never expected to see him again so it has thrown me a bit.' She blinked. 'Okay. I first met Pascal in Paris when we were students together at Barone Fine Chocolate. It was fantastic.' She leant forward and rested her elbows on her knees. 'The best eight months of my life. No doubt about that.'

'So you worked with Pascal? That's amazing.' Then Max frowned and looked at her quite quizzically. 'Wait a minute—why was Pascal training at Barone? I thought he was one of the Barone family?'

'He is. Chef Barone is the fifth generation of Barone chocolatiers, but he was looking for someone to take over the business. Pascal is his nephew, but it turned out that he was way more interested in the business side than the cooking.'

She turned slightly in her chair so that she was closer to Max.

'But he got lucky. I was the other apprentice. He soon found out that I had always been happy to work in the background rather than seeking the limelight. I accepted that—after all, he was the nephew of my boss, and I was just the daughter of a baker from a small village in England. I was just Daisy Flynn. Wannabe chocolatier.'

She looked up at Max, who was staring at her with rapt attention.

'I'm quiet and shy and I always have been. Oh, I have worked hard to overcome it these past three years. But old habits are hard to break. Even now I feel a lot more comfortable in the kitchen than talking to customers.' She shrugged and lifted her chin. 'Pascal knew that from the start. The plan was that I would stay on and take over as master chocolatier in a couple of years. But we had bigger plans. Much bigger. Our idea was to develop a range of chocolates and petit-fours which would be sold to the local hotel trade and expand the shop. It sounded wonderful—so wonderful that I spent every night for weeks working and working on the perfect chocolates which were so unique and so delicious and bound to be a success. Pascal was thrilled, and was so was his uncle. We had everything going for us. And...' Daisy faltered and gave a low sigh. 'Pascal threw in an extra incentive for me to stay. A very personal one.'

She looked down as Max made gentle circles on the back of her hand.

'It will probably come as no surprise to you that after six months I had a crush on Pascal Barone the size of a small planet.' She gave a slight snort. 'You have to remember that I had arrived straight from catering college in one of the most romantic cities in the world, where I worked every day to produce chocolates and pastries for lovers to buy. Then one Saturday evening the shop was closed, the sun was shining, and Pascal asked me out for a drink. We had been working all day, it was April, and the trees were in blossom. So I said yes.'

She allowed herself a wistful sigh.

'A week later I was officially his doting girlfriend, and I finally had a chance to see Paris as it should be seen. With the person you are totally besotted with. It was a magical time. I was so in love with that man and the wonderful future we were going to have together, working side by side for Barone.'

Max exhaled loudly. 'Congratulations. At this point I have to tell you that I'm beginning to feel slightly nauseous at how sweet all this is. Paris in the spring? Okay. I get that. So what happened next?' he asked. 'Why are you not in Paris as the master chocolatier for Barone Fine Chocolate? You were working together as partners, and from what I'm hearing you made a great team.'

'What happened was that life kicked me in the shins and reminded me not to have such delusions of grandeur. My dad was diagnosed with a brain tumour and was given six months to live. So of course I came home.'

'Oh, no. I am so sorry. That must have been traumatic.'

'It was. Dad came to Paris to spend a whole month with me, and we had the most wonderful time together. Pascal charmed him, Chef

Barone took us all to the most amazing restaurants all over Paris, we worked in the shop together and we talked and talked. But at the end I knew I had to come home back to England and be with him for as long as I could.'

'Why do I get the idea that your great plans didn't work out quite the way you expected after all?' Max said in a low voice.

'Back in our small house, we both knew that every second we spent together was precious. And we had fun. Just lots and lots of ridiculous fun. The very best bit was cooking together. Really cooking. Whatever we wanted. It was a different world from Paris—but I loved it.'

Her head dropped and her fingers gripped Max's palm a little tighter.

'It was so very hard to see him fade away in such a short time. I wanted every day to be longer and I felt so guilty for being ambitious. I tried to talk to him about it—he simply kept telling me that he loved me, that the last thing he wanted me to do was move back and take over the bakery and live *his* life. A life in which he had compromised his own ambitions to make a secure home for his family. I had been given the chance to make the most of my skills—but most of all he wanted me to be happy. I had a wonderful, exciting new life and a boyfriend we both adored back in Paris. I had everything he had ever wanted me to have.'

Daisy slipped her hands away from Max and strolled over to the stone balustrade, gazing out over the gardens where the sun was now setting over the tall oak trees.

It took a few seconds for Max to rise and stand alongside her, but her eyes faced forward as she whispered, 'After he died, I found out that he had known about the diagnosis for months but had decided not to tell me. Because he knew that I would want to come back and be with him instead of living my dream life. *His* dream life. In Paris. He loved me so very much, you see. That's why he sold the bakery to a dough-nut chain before he came over to Paris to see me. He was cutting off my escape route back to the life he had known. I had nowhere else to go but forward. But you know what? It just made me so sad. To think that he knew that he had a terminal illness while I was sitting with

Pascal in pavement cafés, drinking coffee in the sunshine.'

Daisy felt Max wrap his arms around her waist so that she could lean back against his chest, confident that he could take her weight. The warmth of his body was so comforting that she almost cried with the delight of it.

'I felt so guilty, Max. And so very, very selfish.'

Max leant his chin on her shoulder and tightened his grip around her waist in an all-embracing girdle of support.

'But that was his decision. He wanted his little girl to be happy. As a father I can understand that. I would probably do the same myself. He must have been a remarkable man.'

'I know. He was. A very remarkable man. The more I thought about it, the more I realised how much he had sacrificed to make a home and a secure life for me—especially after my mother died and there were just the two of us. He could have moved to a restaurant job, but the wages are so low even then he believed it would be impossible. He gave up his dreams for me. And that crushed me, Max. It totally crushed me.'

She shook her head and sucked in a few breaths of cooling air, trying to soothe her burning throat.

'You needed time to grieve,' Max replied, in a voice as soft as the gentle breeze that wafted onto the terrace. 'How did you cope with your loss? Did you go back to Paris and become a demon in the Barone kitchen? Throw yourself back into your work?'

'No. That was just the problem. I was paralysed. I didn't know what to do! I lost interest in food. I lost my passion. My mojo. My zest for the crazy life I had been living, where I'd spent my whole day surrounded by chocolate in every possible form and heaven was working out the exact proportions of hazelnuts and cream and sugar for my praline mousse. All of that work and that life just didn't seem relevant or important any more. My dad had shown me how futile it could be to tie yourself down to one place and let your dreams slip away through your fingers. But the very thing I'd thought I wanted held no attraction for me any longer.'

She lifted both hands and dropped them down to curl around the edge of the cool stone.

'The only thing I knew for sure was that Pascal was still in Paris, waiting for me. So one morning I just threw my bag into the car and headed off to France. All along the way I started building up this wonderful picture of my new life with Pascal, and all the plans we had made about opening up new shops and new markets for the wonderful chocolates I had come up with.' She clenched her fist. 'What an idiot I was.'

'What happened? Had things changed while you were away?'

Daisy nodded slowly. 'Oh, yes, things had changed. I arrived late at night, after driving all day, and expected my loving boyfriend to be waiting for me with open arms. I hadn't told him I was coming. It was meant to be a lovely surprise after he had begged me to come back soon because he was missing me so much. And it was a surprise, all right. I won't bore you with the sordid details, but let's just say that contrary to all his desperate telephone calls, telling me how much he missed me, he was not sleeping alone. The new student at his uncle's shop was prettier and richer than me, and he had simply moved another besotted female into his apartment to take my place.'

Daisy shook her head. 'She was even wearing the same bracelet that he had given me for my birthday. I simply couldn't believe it.'

Max was silent as Daisy blinked away foolish tears for something she'd thought she had lost but in fact had never had in the first place.

'What did you do?'

'Do? I did the one thing he had not expected me to do. I made a huge scene. I ranted, I raved, I cried and screamed, and then I flung all my things into my suitcase while he made excuses along the lines that it was all *my* fault for leaving him on his own for three months just when he needed me most to help build his new business empire.'

She looked up and blinked hard.

'I remember standing outside the apartment in the dark with a suitcase and a couple of plastic carrier bags, feeling as though the world had been whipped away under my feet. People were walking along the pavement and I couldn't believe that they could go about their lives and still be happy when my life was falling apart around me.'

'That must have been a low point.'

She nodded. 'I was too exhausted to drive anywhere, so I spent the night in a local hotel and went to see Chef Barone the next morning. After all, I still had a job and I owed it to my boss to keep my promises. But Pascal had taken with him every one of the new recipes I had come up with for our wonderful new joint venture, and all of his uncle's most popular desserts. And claimed that they were his own work.'

She shook her head.

'His uncle was furious and felt totally betrayed. I was a mess. But what could I do? I was a student, and his uncle was an honourable man who was not going to destroy the family by suing his own nephew. This was exactly what Pascal had expected. The family knew, of course—but Pascal was their golden charmer, who could do no wrong in their eyes. It was simply business. Nothing personal.'

She sniffed.

'Nothing personal. If Pascal only knew how

very angry he made me when he said that to my face.'

'Angry because he had stolen your work and was passing it off as his own? Or angry that he had cheated on you?' Max asked.

Daisy pressed the side of her cheek against Max's face and took hold of his arms, locking his body against hers. 'Both. But most of all I was angry that I had allowed myself to be used by a professional con man like Pascal Barone. He never loved me. He saw that I was a shy, quiet girl who was in Paris for the first time on her own, and that I was talented enough to create something he could use for his own benefit. He used me to get what he wanted. Then dumped me when he had everything he needed to go out on his own.'

'Isn't that a bit harsh? Don't hit me. But you could have laughed in his face and tied him up with lawyers at the first mention of a partnership.'

'Have you never been in love, Max? Have you never trusted someone so much that you would give your life for them in a heartbeat? Can you understand that? Understand what it is like to be so infatuated that you see only the good and the best in the other person? So in love that you could never even imagine a time when your lover would let you down or not want to be with you? Have you?'

Max froze as the impact of each word of Daisy's question washed over him, penetrating his heart and his mind with such ferocity that he had to pause for a second to pull himself together before answering.

Oh, he knew what that felt like. He knew only too well.

He had been totally blown away from the moment he'd seen Kate walking up the long curved road that led to the plantation house on that hot, sultry January afternoon all those years ago.

She'd been wearing a simple white sun top, and tiny shorts which had displayed her stunning long model-perfect legs in all their glory. She might as well have been an alien creature, dropped into his life from outer space.

And he had been totally dazzled.

So dazzled that the thought of what their lives were going to be like going forward had never even crossed his mind. Of *course* she would have to adjust to life in a hot climate, in a rambling old family house with little in the way of luxury and modern conveniences.

They'd loved each other and that was all that mattered—they would find a way to make it work. Kate had loved the beach and her life in the sun.

The fact that he had only known her for a few weeks hadn't been important. They had a lifetime to get to know one other. Why wait to start their married life together? They had nothing to worry about, did they?

Max lifted his chin and tried to keep the sadness from his voice when he replied. This was Daisy's story. She needed his support right now—not to hear about the mistakes he had made in his need to bring love into his life.

'Yes. I know exactly what you are talking about. I was married for three years before I started to realise the difference between infatuation with a dazzling human being and real love, and what that means when you are struggling to hold your marriage together. Good and bad.'

'What do you mean?'

'Kate walked into my life in January and we were married in the June. The weeks in between were like a total whirlwind, with no time to think about the small print. When Kate met me she thought that life on an island in the Caribbean was going to be like one long extended beach holiday. Three years later she was a young mother, with a husband who was working every hour of the day on the estate just to pay the bills. That is a lot for someone so young to handle.'

Daisy half turned in the circle of his arms and looked up at him with such wide-eyed pain and sadness that his heart melted.

'Then you understand. But I thought...' She faltered, and seemed to swallow hard before pressing her forehead against his chest so that he could not see her tears.

'You thought?' he encouraged, and moved his hands higher up her back.

'I thought that I was going to spend the rest of my life with Pascal—working with him side by side to create a chain of remarkable artisan chocolate shops. Of course I trusted him.

I adored him. And he used me. He broke my heart. And I will never forgive him for that.' She gave Max a wavering smile. 'I thought that I was the only one who had made a fool of myself when it came to love. Looks like I was wrong about that.'

She blinked away tears of anger and pain.

'But do you know the worst part? Just seeing Pascal again brings back all my old feelings of not being good enough. It's infuriating that he can still suck away my self-confidence like that.'

'Then don't let him get away with it. You have just as much right to be here as anyone else. More. You have learnt your craft the hard way. The way I see it, your apprenticeship is well and truly over, Miss Flynn. It is your time to take your place with the master chocolatiers. And don't you dare forget that. Especially when it comes to one Pascal Barone,' Max replied, with a fierce smile that made her heart sing. 'You *know* you can work your magic with this contest. Team Barone won't stand a chance against the mighty power of Team Treveleyn.'

'I don't know, Max. Pascal wasn't joking

about the work involved in this competition. He will have the best team in Paris cooking up a storm tomorrow. I really am sorry. You have worked so hard, and now I have screwed this up for you. But you still have the conference. The people here will still want to buy your cocoa. Maybe you should focus on that side and leave me to salvage what I can?'

Max startled her by standing up and drawing her to him. 'We're in this together.'

Daisy scanned his face, which was creased with concern and regret, and could not bring herself to disappoint him. But he deserved to hear the truth about how she felt.

She reached up and smoothed the lapels of his jacket, and as he looked down at her in astonishment she looked up into his eyes, pulled him closer towards her and, in a very clear voice, said, 'Pascal knows me. He knows how I work, he knows my recipes, and he knows the kind of desserts I do well. He'll have done something similar to try and cut me out. This party is over for me, Max. I only have a few hours to come up with replacement desserts. And I don't know if I can do it.'

With that she patted him on the lapels, took a long swig from her champagne glass and walked with as much dignity as she could out across the patio towards the entrance to the kitchens.

Only with her small high-heeled steps and his long-legged bounds it only took a moment for Max to catch up with her and stand, hands on hips, blocking her way forward.

'Not running out on me are you, Flynn?' Max asked in a strong accent which matched the pitch of his jaw. Then his voice softened and he stepped forward and took both her hands in his. 'I have news for you. Team Treveleyn is still very much alive and well. I got us into this mess and it's my job to do what I can to get us out. Just tell me what you need me to do.'

Daisy tried to focus on his face, but her eyes were too full of tears. Through a burning throat she forced out a hoarse reply. 'You have to talk to your customers. The estate needs you to sell what you grow. I'll be okay.'

Max slid towards her, and before she knew it she was trapped inside his arms, his hands pressed against the thin fabric of her dress. Her head fell forward, so that when he spoke, the sounds of his words reverberated inside his chest and through the bones of her head.

'You are more important to me than the cocoa beans.'

Hardly believing that he had just said that, Daisy lifted her head and saw his earnest face. And she knew that he meant it.

He stroked her cheek with the most gentle and featherlight stroke, but his blue eyes were focused tight onto hers, bright with smiling energy and excitement. 'All that was in the past, Daisy Flynn. You've come a long way since then. A very long way. I believe in you and your ability. You won't let yourself or me down. You can do this. I know that you can.'

Daisy opened her mouth to call him on that promise—but what she saw in his face at that moment made her question seem petty and insulting. What she saw in those eyes and that expression told her more powerfully than words or a written contract that he meant what he said.

'Time to let the battle commence. Are you ready? Good. Let's go back, then—and we are *so* not going through the kitchens, Barone or no

Barone. Let's do this, Daisy. Let's show them that Team Treveleyn is not so easily thwarted.'

Max shuffled inch by inch across the bedroom carpet in his stockinged feet so as not to wake Daisy. She had fallen asleep, exhausted, in the crook of his arm well past midnight, after many long hours working through every possible gourmet chocolate dessert which could beat the chocolate mousse cake combination which she was convinced Pascal would expect her to make. And so far she'd failed to come up with anything she was happy with.

He sat down slowly on the bottom corner of the bed and watched her as she slept. She was lying on top of the soft bedcover on her side, dressed in an old T-shirt and men's pyjama bottoms which stretched seductively over her lithe body, revealing curves he should probably not be ogling.

But it was no use. He wanted to see her breasts lift and fall under the thin fabric covering her chest. He wanted to run his hands over the long line of her back as it curved away from him. He wanted it so badly he could almost imagine what it would feel like to touch her warm skin from neck to toes with his fingers.

Heat bubbled up, tingling in his hands and neck. His throat was dry, his palms sweaty.

Daisy Flynn was a lovely woman who had seen a lot in her short life. She deserved to be treasured and loved and cared for by someone worthy of her.

And, if there was a queue, he wanted to be the first in the line.

Was he even capable of giving her the love she needed?

Just the thought of loving someone again was hard to get his head around, and yet here he was. Looking at a stunningly lovely woman he had only met a few days earlier—and yet somehow he felt as though he had known her always. She had waltzed into his life and made a place for herself in his heart which had been vacant for a long time.

Like it or not, he was falling in love with her.

He had never expected to feel this way again. Hoped, maybe—but had never expected it to happen. But where did that leave him? Leave *them*? Because, unless he had got it hopelessly wrong, she felt the same way about him. And just the thought that she might care about him made his heart sing.

What could he offer Daisy?

How many times had she told him that her dream was to open her own chocolate shop in the city? That was never going to happen if they got together.

He had sacrificed everything to make the Treveleyn Estate a success, and telling her how he felt now would be the best way to set them both up for years of hard work with little to show for it and a lifetime of regret and broken dreams.

Daisy stirred gently in her sleep and sighed gently as Max looked into her calm, unlined and relaxed face.

Twenty-four hours from now they would be heading back to London and their separate lives. He had Freya's birthday party and Daisy had a full workload with her friend Tara.

And then he had to fly home. Back to St Lucia. Alone.

Without Freya. Without Daisy.

Max shuffled around the woman he loved and

bent down to press the gentlest of kisses on top of her mussed-up hair so that she did not even stir.

His fingers longed to ripple through that hair just as much as his body willed him to slide next to her on the bed and hold her in his arms.

But he couldn't be so selfish. The weight of his past and what she had come to mean to him were too heavy to ignore.

It was time to let Daisy Flynn become the girl who got away. Even if it meant keeping his true feelings locked inside for the short time that they would be together.

He had to let her go. So that she could fly high on her own wings without feeling trapped on an island without the chance to realise her dreams.

So he slowly slid away, his eyes never leaving her face, until he reached the bedroom door and was forced to return to his own room, where he knew that sleep would be impossible.

Because the truth was too hard to take.

He had broken his promise to Daisy. He had let her down.

He pressed the palm of his hand flat against the bedroom door, reluctant to break the con-

nection. Right next to a poster for the hotel
chain's newest hotel. Set in an old tea plantation in the tropical highlands of Sri Lanka.

Strange how the colonial style plantation
house looked so much like his own house on
St Lucia. They had probably been built around
the same time.

According to the poster, the hotel group were
looking for other innovative virgin eco sites,
and were offering eco-tourism, employment,
and guaranteed investment in the local com-
munity.

Max tapped two fingers against the poster.

Maybe he should follow Daisy's example and
take a completely fresh look at how to solve his
problems?

Time to crack open his laptop. He had some
research to do, and he had to do it fast.

CHAPTER TEN

MAX pulled up his chair at the breakfast table in Daisy's bedroom and poured himself a glass of cool, freshly pressed orange and mango juice.

'Oh, I needed that.'

He smiled across the table at Daisy, who was huddled on her chair, both hands clutched around a large beaker of very strong-smelling coffee. She looked exhausted, and had jumped at his suggestion that they take advantage of the room service option rather than face the other contestants over a sumptuous breakfast buffet in the main dining room.

'Have you eaten yet?' he asked, and started cutting into his organic bacon, mushrooms, sausage, poached eggs and fried bread. 'You really should. You need strength, energy—whatever.'

'Do you have hollow legs?' she moaned as he speared a mushroom and popped it into his mouth.

'Who? Me? Just a healthy appetite,' he replied, waving his fork around. 'And you forget that a traditional full English breakfast is hard to find in the Caribbean, unless I make it myself. English bacon and sausage are in very short supply in that part of the world.' He paused, his reloaded fork halfway to his mouth. 'I tried to cook eggs once. I think my housekeeper threw the frying pan away rather than try to clean it. Not a success. How about you? Have you had enough to eat?'

'I'm good. Lots of carbohydrates. Juice. Now all I need is another gallon of coffee and I might stay awake long enough to cook this morning.'

Max put down his fork long enough to spread a generous slice of butter on his toast. 'There have to be some advantages to being in the fifth round. For one, you can watch the first four pairs of contestants and find out how they work—or don't work—before you start yourself.'

She shook her head. 'Too late for that. I handed the conference office my full menu and recipes as soon as it opened at eight this morning. So, unless I have some kind of disaster, I am locked into those three dishes. Only small tweaks are allowed now. That's it,' she said fatalistically, and took another long sip of coffee. 'I am doomed. All that work in the run-up to this competition and I've wiped it out in one huge risky decision. I should probably apologise now and get it over with.'

Max wiped ketchup from his upper lip before sitting back in his chair. Daisy bent over from the waist and banged her forehead twice on the tablecloth before closing her eyes. Her fingers were still clutched around the coffee mug, and Max slowly untangled them one by one.

'Come on,' he said with a smile, as he stood up and walked around the small bedroom table. Before Daisy could complain, he slid one arm under her legs, the other around her waist and lifted her into his arms so fast that pure instinct made her fling her arms around his neck.

'What are you doing?'

'Taking you over to the bed, of course. You need to lie down somewhere comfy while you tell me all about the new dessert you are going to make. Because last time we talked there wasn't much progress on that front.'

He lowered her onto the bedcover, flicked the quilt over her bare feet, and went back to pour himself a coffee before perching on the end of bed and staring at her over the rim of his cup.

'Don't keep me in suspense. What have you come up with? I presume it contains some form of chocolate?' he teased.

Daisy pushed back against the solid wood bedhead and pulled a pillow onto her chest. 'Oh, Max. The more I think about it, the more I think I might have made a horrible mistake. It's just too risky for a contest where so much is riding on the results. I am an idiot. I should have chosen something more conventional.'

Max shook his head from side to side. 'We went through all this at some ridiculously early hour this morning. That's precisely what Pascal and the rest of the competition will be expecting you to do. So—what strange and magical culinary delight have you come up with?'

She exhaled slowly. 'When my dad came to visit me in Paris, Chef Barone spent hours with us almost every evening, eating, drinking and talking—lots of talking. Sharing our love of confectionery and chocolate. On our last evening we cooked a meal together—just the three us. And my dad made this dessert. It only took twenty minutes to bake—but wow! I mean *wow*. Even Chef Barone asked him for the recipe, but he said that it was going to be one of the last things he would ever make after a lifetime of experimenting. He called it a Fleur Delice and it was his legacy to me.'

A single tear slipped from the corner of Daisy's eye and Max passed her a box of tissues from the bedside cabinet. But she had already used the pillowcase.

'Then it must be something very special,' Max replied in a low voice. 'Because if it's good enough for your dad it's good enough for this contest.'

She glanced up at him, then her fingers started making shapes in the quilt by crunching it into tight rolls of fabric.

'That's why I may have made a mistake,' she whispered. 'You see, I've actually only made it once before. It was my dad's birthday, and he was having a lot of problems. We both knew that he had already lived a lot longer than the doctors had expected. This was going to be his last birthday.'

Without saying a word, Max walked slowly around to the other side of the bed, slipped off his shoes and sat on the bed next to Daisy, his back against the bedhead so that his left side was touching her right.

It seemed only natural for her to mesh the fingers of her right hand between his.

She looked up into his face as he stroked the hair back from her forehead in silence, content to listen to her speak although her voice was so thin and strained.

'It was a lovely sunny day, so we ran away to the seaside and walked along the beach and ate fish and chips for lunch. Then I drove us back home for a quiet afternoon watching his favourite movie, to be followed by a meal made up of all of his favourite dishes. With his Fleur Delice to finish. I had just poured the wine and I went to wake him from his nap. And he was gone, Max. He had just slipped away in his sleep.'

The words caught in her throat, and he wrapped his arm around her waist so that her head could fall onto his shoulder.

'When I was on my own that night I ate the Fleur Delice. All of it. Every single mouthful. And it was so amazing. It would probably be a bestseller, but I haven't made it since.'

'Of course you haven't,' Max murmured, his chin pressed against the top of her head. 'It's too special and way too personal for you to serve to your paying customers.'

Daisy closed her eyes and luxuriated in the warmth of his body pressed against her side. Without thinking of the consequences she leant sideways against him, daring to push the boundaries that they had set only a few days earlier.

His left arm snaked down the pillow to her waist and he drew her even closer to his body.

She could feel the pounding of his heart under the smart blue shirt as she pressed her fingertips to the soft fabric which separated his skin from hers, only too aware that one thin layer of mightily creased cotton was not perhaps the best outfit she could have chosen for a breakfast meeting with her cocoa-grower.

Who was she kidding? Max was more to her than that. She had never told anyone about that cake—not even Pascal or Tara, who would have seen it as a marketing opportunity if ever there was one.

Until this week she would never have thought it possible that she could forge so powerful a bond with this amazing man—and feel friendship and that connection back in return.

Pascal had been her lover and her colleague, and for a few idyllic and heady months in one of the most romantic cities in Europe she'd thought they had a future together in Paris—but, looking back, she knew now that Pascal had never been her friend.

Max shuffled even closer to her on the bed and Daisy breathed in a sensory overload of his scent. Cooked breakfast and coffee, of course. Then a spicy citrus-sharp scent—and something else. That subtle aroma of *Max*, which was totally unique—and if she could bottle it she would never need to work again.

It was so intoxicating that she blocked out all the excellent rational reasons why she should not get involved and leant even closer none the less, cuddling against Max's body.

His heart rate increased to match her own heavy breathing, and she could feel his breath on her cheek. Hot. Fast. All linked to the deep feeling of warmth and connection that came from two single consenting adults who liked each other more than a little, lying on a warm soft quilt, in a quiet, sunlit luxury bedroom on a Saturday morning with nothing to do for at least an hour. With the sound of birdsong filtering through the open window.

She could stay this way for ever and not regret it. But just as her head lolled back against the pillow she sensed his mood change—as though someone had opened the window wider and allowed a cool breeze into the room.

His arm slid away from behind her back and he moved just an inch, then more, further along the bedhead. And their bodies slid apart, slowly at first, then more swiftly as Max shuffled off the bed and strolled over to the breakfast table.

The shock of being separated was like a physical blow to Daisy's poor heart. But it was the look on Max's face that truly startled her as he turned to face her.

Anguish, self-reproach—and unmistakable desire. For *her*.

Somewhere deep inside her she knew that Max Treveleyn cared about her. And wanted her.

She had not been mistaken after all. The way his hand had started to seek hers when they were out. The way she caught him looking at her when she least expected it. And that kiss on the patio had been real. The gentleness of his mouth on the nape of her neck which had turned her legs to jelly had meant as much to him as it had to her.

She didn't know whether to grin and shout in glee while she had the chance, or be patient and let him take the lead.

This was why when he did speak the words he used touched her heart and made it weep.

'I can't do this, Daisy. You're a lovely woman, and any man would be honoured to have you in his life, but we both know that I will be back on the island this time next week. It wouldn't be fair on either of us to make promises we can't keep. No matter how much we would like things to be different.'

Well. That answered that question.

Two choices. She could accept what he said

and let him go with a smile on her face—or she could do something mad and challenge him.

Just the thought of not having Max in her life sent a cold shiver down her back. He was hers and nobody else's. She had not even realised that until this moment. She had been through an unhappy love affair with a man who could never have been her friend, and she knew the difference now as clear as night from day.

She did not want to lose Max Treveleyn. She could not lose him—not now, not after all they had shared together.

She wanted Max, and she wanted him badly enough to fight for him.

Unless, of course, he was making excuses to shake her off and she had completely misread the signs?

'Can't do what, Max? Be friends with me? Like me and want to spend time with me? Want to hold me in your arms? Is that what you can't do, Max? Please tell me the truth, because I'm starting to get confused by what your body is telling me and the words actually coming out of your mouth.' Then her voice softened. 'Aren't I good enough for you?' she whispered.

Before Daisy realised what was happening Max had crossed the few steps that separated them and wrapped his hand around the back of her neck. His fingers worked into her hair as he pressed his mouth against hers, pushing open her full lips, moving back and forth, his breath fast and heavy on her face.

His mouth was tender, gentle but firm, as though he was holding back the floodgates of a passion which was on the verge of breaking through and overwhelming them both.

She felt that potential. She trembled at the thought of it. And at that moment she knew that she wanted it as much as he did.

Her eyes closed as she wrapped her arms around his back and leaned into the kiss, kissing him back, revelling in the sensual heat of his body as it pressed against hers. Closer, closer, until his arms were taking the weight of her body, enclosing her in his loving, sweet embrace. The pure physicality of the man was almost overpowering, and the movement of his muscular body pressed against hers, combined with the heavenly scent that she knew now was unique to him alone.

It filled her senses with an intensity that she had never felt in the embrace of any other man in her life. He was totally overwhelming. Intoxicating. Delicious.

Just when Daisy thought that there could be nothing more pleasurable in the world his kiss deepened. It was as though he wanted to take everything she was able to give him, and without a second of doubt she surrendered to the hot spice of the taste of his mouth and tongue. Coffee and chocolate. And Max.

This was the loving, warm kiss she had never known. The connection between them was part of it, but this went beyond friendship and common interests. This was a kiss to signal the start of something new. The kind of kiss in which each of them was opening up their most intimate secrets and deepest feelings for the other person to see.

The heat, the intensity, the desire of this man were all there, exposed for her to see, when she eventually opened her eyes and broke the connection. Shuddering. Trembling.

He pulled away, the faint stubble on his chin

grazing across her mouth as he lifted his face to kiss her eyes, brow and temple.

It took a second for her to catch her breath before she felt able to open her eyes—only to find Max was still looking at her, his forehead still pressed against hers. A smile warmed his face as he moved his hand down to stroke her cheek.

He knew. He knew the effect that his kiss was having on her body. Had to. Her face burned with the heat coming from the point of contact between them. His own heart was racing just as hers was.

'Is that the way you usually silence women who ask you tough questions?' Daisy asked, trying to keep her voice casual and light. And failing.

He simply smiled a little wider in reply, one side of his mouth turning up more than the other, before he answered in a husky voice, 'I save it for emergencies. And for when I need to answer tough questions.'

Max pulled back and looked at her, eye to eye.

'Don't you dare even think that you are not good enough. You have to know that it is killing me to even consider leaving you here when

I head back home next week, but that is where I live. I tried commuting between Britain and St Lucia before, and I come back to see Freya whenever I can, but it is so hard, Daisy. So very hard. You deserve a lot better than a part time lover.'

'Hmm?' He was nuzzling the side of her head now, his lips moving over her brow and into her hair as she spoke. 'Do I? I think that is the nicest thing that anyone has ever said to me.'

'And I mean every word. Your life is here, where you have a brilliant future in retail. I can see it now. Not in some grotty house in the middle of nowhere in the West Indies.'

'I think you are forgetting something very important here, Mr Treveleyn. This is me you're talking to. Miss Entrepreneur. Don't they have wonderful luxury hotels on your island? And don't those hotels need dessert chefs who can work with local chocolate producers? And what about your cocoa? Wouldn't you like to see it made into finished chocolate closer to home? Just think—the tourist board would probably make you an offer you couldn't refuse if your chocs were bringing in tourists by the plane-load.'

She was giggling now, and waving her arms about.

'We have more options working together than we could ever have imagined. If you're willing to give us a chance. This is our opportunity to be together, Max. Why won't you let me be with you? Let me love you? Tell me, because I really do want to know.'

She was instantly rendered speechless as Max replied by cupping her face in his hands and running his thumbs across both her damp cheeks.

'Why? Because I don't feel good enough for you, Daisy Flynn. Not nearly good enough. Does that answer your question?'

He was serious. Max actually thought that he was not worthy of her.

Daisy sighed out loud, then tried to shake her head—but he was holding it like a precious china vase.

'Of all the ridiculous things I have ever heard, that takes some beating. For a sensible man you do talk nonsense, Max Treveleyn. Look at what you have achieved on the estate. What was it like when you took over? And now you are here, at this conference, with a world-beating chocolate any chef would be proud to use. I know I am.'

He smiled and flicked her fringe back, apparently fascinated by her unruly bed-hair. 'You are? That's good to know. But it doesn't get away from the fact that I am struggling to pay wages while you are on the up. I am *not* going to be responsible for another woman's pain and disappointment.'

Ah. At last.

Daisy took hold of his clever, sensitive fingers, which were doing amazing things to her hormone levels when she was trying to say something sensible, and clasped them tight inside her own.

'From what you tell me Kate had a lovely dream of an idea that her life on the plantation would be one long beach holiday. It wasn't, and I am sorry for that—but, hey, I like cocoa. You may have noticed this?'

'Maybe I have.' Max grinned, then his smile faded and he shook his head. 'But it doesn't change the fact that there are times when I wish my little girl could be proud of her old dad. It's hard spending time apart. And things are going to get even harder when Kate remarries. I want to be there for Freya when she needs me.' He flicked his head back. 'Things are going to have to change—and soon.'

'Oh, Max. I haven't met Freya, but I can tell you something. My dad gave up his dreams and his happiness so that I'd have the finances to go to catering college. He had so many wonderful ideas that he never saw through before he died. Don't make the same mistake. I mean it. Freya loves you for who you are. Not because you own a cocoa plantation. She would never want you to give up your dreams for her. *Never.* I know. I've been there. So don't you even think about selling up—okay?'

Max paused, and his wonderful blue eyes looked into hers with an expression of astonishment and recognition.

'I knew I'd made the right choice that day at the food fair. You are right. You are *so* right and you have just helped me to make a decision. I am going to do something rash.'

'Rash? What do you mean rash? Max?'

'I've had a crazy idea about how to turn my plantation around, but I need to speak to a lot of people before I know whether it's even feasible or not. Heck, have you seen the time? I have a whole twenty minutes to get changed before my presentation starts. Then it's back-to-back meetings for the rest of the day.'

Daisy was about to reply but never got the chance. Max crushed his mouth onto hers in a kiss which left her breathless and reeling.

'I know you can't take phones into the kitchens, but I will be hovering around the main conference all day if you need me. Okay?' he said as he practically jogged to the door, snatching a breakfast muffin as he went. 'I'll explain everything later. Bye. And, Daisy...?' He stopped and looked at her from the open doorway. 'Go and show them how it's done. I know that you can do it. That's my girl.' And with a cheeky wink he was gone and the door closed behind him.

Daisy pulled a pillow over her head.

Men. How did she get herself into these situations?

* * *

It was after six that Saturday evening before Daisy finally managed to make it back to her hotel room—and only then because the head chef had physically taken the icing bag out of her hand, after she had spent ten minutes walking back and forwards, staring at the decorated dessert plates, adding a dot or an extra swirl, not daring to leave until they were as stunning to look at as she could possibly make them.

It had been almost painful to see her finished plates being whisked away by the waiters into the judging room, knowing that there was nothing she could do now to change the work and it was all up to the judges to make their decision.

It was not going to be easy. The kitchen had been organised so that the other contestant was working on the opposite bench. They'd faced away from one other and it had been impossible to peek at what the other chef was making. But judging from the delicious smells of toasted coconut, passion fruit and mango, the charming middle-aged chef from Ghana, who had chatted to her so calmly outside the kitchen for almost an hour as they'd waited to go in, was clearly working on a tropical theme.

Perhaps she should have done the same? Especially with chocolate from the West Indies?

The new dessert had been finished by four that afternoon, and it was the best chocolate cake that she had ever made. Her hands had seemed to move automatically as she'd folded in the cream and chocolate to make the light and elegant, delicate and frothy sabayon base.

Simple ingredients—the best that she could find.

So, so good.

But it was more than that.

For the whole hour or so that it had taken to make the cake batter she'd felt as though her dad was standing next to her at the kitchen bench, chatting away, tasting and testing, lining the baking tray, checking the temperature. Relaxed, calm, and happy that at last the culmination of so many years of work was finally being put to use in such a spectacular setting.

It had been totally crazy, but somehow magical and special at the same time.

With her dad by her side, smiling and encouraging, even the discreet TV crews had not bothered her in the least.

Of course she had tasted a tiny sliver of the cake—she'd simply had to. It was every bit as good as she remembered, and it looked terrific. *Thank you, Dad.*

But now it was all over. She had finished.

She had taken the challenge and worked harder than she had ever worked—she had done the very best she could to show how marvellous Trevelyn Estate chocolate could be.

No going back. No last-minute changes. All she could do now was wait for the after-dinner speeches.

Daisy collapsed down onto the silky cover of her luxurious super-soft bed and fell back with her arms out on either side as the stress and adrenaline of the past twenty-four hours hit her hard.

She raised one arm and squinted at her watch. Drinks were scheduled for seven, and then she would have to tuck into a four-course meal complete with rich, creamy and chocolatey sauces, made by the hotel chef, and a selection of the contestants' desserts before the judges made their final announcements.

Assuming, of course, that she would be able

to eat anything at all. She felt way too nervous to eat food cooked by someone else.

Of course Max and Tara would both tell her that she was overreacting.

She would be okay. What was the big deal about strolling into a ballroom full of elegant and beautiful aristocratic people who came to this sort of splendid hotel several times a week?

Thank heavens she would have Max by her side.

She shuffled up the bed and picked up her cell phone from the bedside table. She had been so tempted to slip out of the preparation room that afternoon and catch a few words of encouragement from Max, but she'd known that he was way too much of a distraction at precisely the time when she needed to focus on what she was doing.

And he had needed space to deal with his problems in his own way.

She held the phone with both hands over her head, scanned through two good luck messages from Tara and...there it was. Max had sent her a text message every hour, on the hour, during the whole day. His speech had gone well, he had serious customers, and he missed her. And then she noticed a voicemail from Max, sent around the same time as she had been standing outside the kitchens, palms sweating and mouth dry, ready to start.

Perhaps it was to tell her that he wasn't coming back and she would have to deal with this on her own after all? Or that he had signed a wonderful deal with one of the major chocolate manufacturers he had been chatting to most of the previous day instead?

Oh, just listen to the recorded message and get it over with, you silly girl!

She pressed the button and Max bellowed out from her phone, sounding as though he was either in the car or running. Either way, just the crackly sound of his voice made her lie back on the pillow so that she could bathe in his words, savouring each one in turn.

'Hi! I hoped to catch you before you started cooking. Instead of which I am walking in the sunshine on the way to meeting number four. So here goes—this is what I would say in my clumsy way if I was able to stand next to you right now. I am only a poor cocoa farmer, and you have only been in my life for a short time, but I know this: I know that you are remarkable, beautiful and talented beyond measure. I know that I believe in you, and I know that I could not have chosen a better chocolatier to work with. You will always do your very best. So be ready to get out there and be audacious. Because the world deserves to see your beautiful light. It is time for you to come out of the kitchen, Daisy, and let that dazzling light break through the darkness. Both of us have been living under a shadow for far too long.

'My meetings are running late—but I will be there to escort you into dinner. And whatever the judges decide we have already won. Because you know now that you are capable of achieving anything you set your heart on. So no more settling for second-hand dreams, Daisy Flynn. You can do anything. Anywhere you want. This is your life, so get ready to have a brilliant evening—and I'll see you around seven. Oh—and I won't get lost. Your dazzling light will be my beacon.'

Daisy lay still for a few minutes, eyes closed, with the telephone clasped to her chest. She was listening, just listening, to the sound of the world that was spinning all around her. Birdsong from the lovely grounds outside her bedroom window, lively chatter and laughter from a cluster of men in the corridor, and the sound of her own breathing as tears trickled down her cheeks.

Crazy, foolish, wonderful man! What was he doing, leaving her messages like that?

Wow, was she grateful that she had not picked up his message before she went into the kitchen—because if she had there would have been a very weepy girl crying into her egg whites while trying to read her own recipes and failing.

Max believed in her! Thought that she was capable of achieving anything. Doing anything. What was the term he had used? Second-hand dreams? Oh, yes, she knew about those.

Daisy rolled sideways and off the edge of the bed, the phone still clasped in her hand. From here she could see her reflection in the mirror glass of the wardrobe.

Ever since she had got back from Paris, and the humiliation of being taken for granted by

Pascal, her one goal had been to open her own chocolate shop. She had told everyone from Tara to the chefs she worked with all over London that in two years, three at most, she would have her own place in the city. Her name over the door. Her brand.

But now, sitting here, it hit her—and hit her hard—that Max had seen through her claims and protests. She wanted to open a shop because that was what her father had wanted—and he'd never got the chance. He'd been a loving, caring, talented man, and she'd adored him, but she knew that he could have cut back on the bakery and spent more time on his chocolate work. He hadn't been brave enough to make the move.

Oh, Dad. She would be a poor example of a daughter if she didn't make the most of every second of her life. She loved her work. She loved seeing the look of exquisite pleasure on the faces of complete strangers when they tasted the food she created. Those were the things that gave her joy and satisfaction. Not money in the bank or a big banner over a shop door—but real happiness, with people she loved around her.

Max was right. She was still living in her father's shadow. And it was finally time to step out of the kitchen and into the light.

She *did* have choices. A bewildering selection of choices, if she was truly honest. And being with Max on a tropical island had suddenly shot right to the top of the list.

What she did and where she did it was still up for grabs.

A shocking and totally exhilarating idea swished around inside her brain. She did not need to spend her whole life tied to a single retail outlet on some city street to express her creative talent—she could do that anywhere she chose.

But there was one thing she was absolutely clear about. She knew now exactly who she wanted to spend her life with. Maximilian Treveleyn. The man she had only met a few days ago. The man she was totally in love with. The man she was ready and willing to fight for. And if that meant learning to be a farmer on an island in the Caribbean—well, that was what she was going to have to do. Because she was not letting him go. No second best for her. Not any more.

She was free.

For the first time in way too many long years she felt able to simply live in the moment and enjoy where she was and what she was doing. Not fighting or working or running from one place to the next with orders and deliveries. And free from Pascal and the pain of the past.

Tonight she was finally going to be herself.

Max was right. She had done everything she possibly could to impress the judges, and the recipes she had chosen represented the essence of who she was. Even the dessert cake was a triumph she would never have been brave enough to try without the superb organic chocolate that Max had created. There was nothing more to do but enjoy this lovely hotel and come out of the kitchen into the world.

She felt lighter. Almost as if the weight of responsibility for living the life she had planned with her father years ago had been lifted from her shoulders.

Daisy stopped, closed her eyes, and slowly, slowly exhaled.

She should be scared. Frightened of being cast loose onto an open sea of bewildering opportunities. But she wasn't scared in the least. She could work anywhere she wanted. Go anywhere. Have fun. And just that one single thought made her dizzy with excitement and joy.

Daisy started unbuttoning her jacket. What was she doing, sitting in her room! She had a party to get ready for.

It was time to start living her life.

CHAPTER ELEVEN

'DADDY, your little tie thing is all twisted.' Freya sighed and stood on the bed so that she could tug at it, both lips pressed together tight with concentration.

'It is? Thank goodness your mummy brought you to see me at this nice hotel. Otherwise I would have had to go down to an extra-special posh awards dinner with a crooked tie,' Max replied, his neck already hurting from bending down so much. 'And that would never do, would it? How's that? Am I done?'

She nodded, and was rewarded by a big smoochy kiss as Max swung her up into the air, making her squeal.

'Hey, what's all this noise about?' Kate asked from the bathroom.

'Mummy, come and look at Daddy. He's got his bestest suit on and *everything*.'

'So he has.' Kate stuck her head out of the

bathroom door and nodded several times before pointing towards Max. 'Don't you think he looks smart? Your clever daddy is going to be a wonderful hotel manager and sell lots of cocoa beans. And then we are all going to go to the island to see him, and stay for the whole of the Christmas holidays. How about that?'

'Yay! Clever Daddy. When can we go, Daddy? Tomorrow? Can we go tomorrow?'

'Hey! Hold on there, gorgeous,' Max replied, as Freya flung her arms around his neck. 'I am going to build a few extras onto the house first, so that it's nice and cool for you all the time, and you can swim and play all day long. Can I tell you what the best bit is? I have to whisper it.'

She leant forward so that her ear and most of her party dress was pressed against his face, making breathing a challenge.

'The best bit is that I get to be with my little girl for a whole Christmas holiday—but this time on the beach in hot sunshine. With real parrots and bananas you can pick straight from the bush. And boats and sailing and lots of jungle creatures to find. It is going to be mega.'

Freya's eyes widened. '*Mega*. You are the bestest daddy in the whole world.'

Max looked over towards Kate as he hugged Freya so tight that she squealed, and Kate winked back as he mouthed silent thanks.

'It's time to let your dad go and talk to the grown-ups and be a very important business person while we finish getting dressed. Five more minutes, then we can skip down and join the party. Okay?'

Freya slid down Max's dinner suit and gave a huge shrug. 'Five whole minutes? Okay. See you soon, Daddy. You have to go and be important now.'

'See you soon.' Max tapped the end of her nose with his fingertip. 'See you very soon.'

Max practically slid along the marble floor at the hotel reception desk, and had to hold onto the counter to steady himself.

Was he in time? He had to be. He simply had to be! He would never forgive himself if he was late for the conference dinner and let Daisy down just when she needed him to be there.

Stretching up on tiptoe, he looked over the

heads of the people who were wandering out of the cocktail lounge towards the splendid dining room.

There she was.

Chatting to the managing director of the company who owned this entire chain of boutique eco hotels. The elegantly dressed Austrian was clearly delighted at something she was saying, and as Max watched in awe the man actually threw his head back and laughed out loud, startling the contest judges who were gathering at the top table near the dais.

Max blinked and shook his head for a second, before smiling across at her. His heart was racing just to see her beautiful face.

Daisy.

She was wearing a black cocktail dress, smiling and laughing like a total networking professional, with one of the most influential and most recognised hoteliers in the world, as though this was something she did every day of the week.

What happened to the girl he had met only a few days ago, who had steadfastly refused to come out of the kitchen and recognise her own talent and excellence? Now she looked relaxed. In control and comfortable in such exalted company.

A large lump ached in his throat. He was so proud of her. Proud of everything she had achieved. No matter what happened with the contest, Daisy was the winner. He could see it in everything about her—the way she held her body, the way she smiled and laughed with her hands flying about everywhere. She was stunning. And happy.

His Daisy was happy.

He sucked in a long breath and lifted his head as he made his way around the edge of the crowded dining room towards her. Constant interruptions and greetings from fellow growers and conference delegates who had made him so welcome only the day before blocked his path at every step, and it seemed to take hours instead of minutes to finally reach the spot where she had been standing.

He suppressed the joyous bubble of happiness that came from the special spot deep inside his chest which he had thought frozen, never to be thawed again. But that had been before he'd laid eyes on this strange, quirky little red-haired girl who was a source of constant change and excitement. She had whipped away the carpet from below his feet the moment he had seen her standing behind the counter at the food festival, and he still felt as though he was walking on quicksand.

With this girl he never knew what to expect from one minute to the next!

And he loved it.

Time to let her know that he had arrived.

'Daisy,' he whispered, and she spun around—then froze.

Her eyes widened as he gazed straight at her, the heat of the blush on her cheeks matching the warmth of the smile that turned up both sides of her mouth.

Her hair was down, her make-up a slick of mascara and a lipgloss that was mostly deposited on the wine glass she was holding in her hand, and yet the look in those eyes as they smiled at him across the group of people that strolled between them told him everything he needed to know.

It was as though the spirit of the girl who was Daisy Flynn was shining through for him alone.

She was totally dazzling, making every other woman appear dull and lifeless and without talent or sparkle.

She was totally, devastatingly beautiful.

Forget the contest, forget the crowds, and forget the hotel managing director, who had given him a wave before moving back towards the judging table. All that mattered was Daisy. He needed to talk to her and share his exciting news. He simply wanted to be with her.

She took a step forward, her eyes never leaving his.

'I got your message. And I decided to take your advice and come out of the kitchen and enjoy myself. Thank you. You're late, by the way.'

'You're most welcome. And I'm sorry for being late. You look...beautiful.'

Her mouth widened into a grin so wide it blocked out the rest of the room. He had never seen her grin like that before, and if a few simple words from him were capable of having that effect then he would have to repeat them again and again, until she knew that they were true.

'Then you are totally forgiven,' she replied, biting her lower lip.

She slid closer and reached out to flick an imaginary piece of fluff from his jacket, then pressed the palms of her hands against his chest.

'I was beginning to think you were going to stand me up, Max Treveleyn.'

'Me? Never. There were things I needed to do before I could start my new life with the woman I love.'

Her eyes widened in shocked surprise, but before she could reply Max took the initiative and slipped his hands onto her waist, his gaze never leaving her lovely face.

'You've stolen my heart, Daisy Flynn,' he whispered across the tiny space that separated them. 'I want to spend the rest of my life showing you just how much I love you.'

'On St Lucia?' Daisy replied, her forefinger tracing a gentle circle on his cheek.

'Possibly. Apparently this hotel chain is considering a wonderful new location on that particular island which was offered to them only today. On an organic cocoa plantation, of all places. Imagine that? It will be an eco project which will guarantee tourism and jobs and sell lots and lots of cocoa. But our home doesn't have to be there. I love St Lucia, and I know you could too, but your happiness means everything to me. I don't want to make the same mistake again. Just tell me where you want to go and I will take you there. My home is where you are, Daisy. On St Lucia, or in London, or Paris, or wherever else you want to go.'

Daisy touched both sides of his face with her fingertips, tears glistening in her amazing green eyes.

'Then take me home with you. To St Lucia.'

Max blinked several times as the impact of what she was saying hit home.

'You astonish me. No wonder I love you.'

'And I thought you were only after me for my chocolate boobs,' she teased.

'Oh, a lot more than that,' he retorted lovingly.

Stepping into the circle of his arms, Daisy wrapped her arms around his neck, stood on tiptoe and kissed him. Lovingly, longingly, deeply. Completely ignoring the hoots and cheers from the other diners at this prestigious conference, and calls about their finding a room.

'Daddy! Daddy! I'm over here, Daddy.'

Daisy whipped around just in time as a slim little blonde girl in a pink party dress propelled herself out of the crowd and wrapped her arms like a limpet around Max's thigh.

'Hey, look who made it just in time for dinner,' Max said as he hoisted her up into his arms. 'It's the lovely Freya. Have you left your mum behind somewhere?'

The little girl nodded and pointed in the direction of the entrance. 'Mummy had to talk to a man about the car, but I couldn't wait to see you, Daddy. I couldn't wait one minute more.'

'Well, I'm so glad you're here, poppet.' Max grinned and rubbed his nose against Freya's, making her giggle. 'Because there is someone I want you to meet. Do you remember what I said to you earlier? About the pretty lady who is baking lovely cakes with the chocolate I make? Well, here she is. This is Freya, my little girl. And, Freya, this is Daisy, who is going to be your new stepmother.'

Freya, of course, immediately tried to bury her head in her father's shoulder.

'Freya's pretending to be shy right now, but

you wait and see what happens when the chocolate cake comes out. Oh, yes.'

Freya peeked out at Daisy, who smiled back at her, and something must have worked because then Freya sniffed and declared to the world in a loud voice, 'My daddy is the best daddy in the whole world, and he makes the bestest chocolate. And I am going to stay at his house on the island and see where the chocolate comes from and everything.'

Daisy nodded wisely. 'You are obviously an expert, because I completely agree with you. He *does* make the bestest chocolate in the world. I think that's why I love him so much.'

'You do?' Freya asked, wide-eyed. 'Cool.' And she gave Daisy a huge toothy grin.

'Oh yes,' Daisy replied with a nod. Then she blinked at Max. 'Did you just say stepmother? I can't be a stepmother. I'm twenty-eight. It's against the law to be a stepmother at twenty-eight. Don't I need some kind of specialist training for the role? It could be risky.'

'Very. But I'm tempted to take the risk if you are,' Max said, leaning towards her, tempted once again by her glorious lips.

'Dad! Stop kissing Daisy. This is *so* embarrassing.'

'Sorry, sweetie. That's something you are going to have to get used to.'

EPILOGUE

DAISY snatched a calming breath of the warm perfumed breeze as Tara checked for the third time in fifteen minutes that Daisy's coronet of fragrant frangipani blossom, jasmine and pale yellow orchids was not in danger of going *anywhere* soon, before running out to try and track down Freya, who had hit the coral-tinged beach running an hour ago and not been seen since.

The heavy silk of Daisy's cream embroidered dress rustled as she strolled out of the shade of the snowy white canopy and looked out across the azure water in the bay to the dark green peaks of the Piton volcanoes that made St Lucia one of the most beautiful islands in the West Indies. A steel drum orchestra was already playing under the shade of the palm trees that lined the sandy beach, filling the air with bright, happy music which blended with the laughter from the wedding guests who were making their way out of the Treveleyn Estate Hotel, where the reception was going to be held.

The Flynn-Treveleyn wedding was going to be the hotel's first beach wedding—which was only fitting, since the hotel was still being constructed around Max's old plantation house.

A lump the size of a pineapple formed in Daisy's throat.

She had come a long way from that baker's shop in a small country town in rural England to stand here today, surrounded by views so dazzling that even after seven months on the island she was still stunned on a daily basis that she was able to make her home in this lovely place, and with people who had taken her to their hearts.

She wished that her parents were here today to share her happiness—they would have loved it here so much. Loved Max and Freya and her new friends. Loved the life that she was making for herself because of all that they had given her.

The sound of a powerful boat engine drew her attention back to the ocean and the sun-bleached white jetty, and Daisy's breath caught in her throat as Max pulled a beautiful speed-boat dressed in white ribbons to a gentle halt.

Next to him on the soft leather seat were Kate and her fiancé, Anton, who had sailed their yacht into the nearby harbour four days ago as part of their very special wedding present. Daisy and Max were going to spend a week sailing the islands on the luxury yacht, while Kate and Anton roughed it with Freya in one of the new eco-cabins the hotel chain had built on the plantation estate.

If you could call a three-bedroom, solar-powered cabin built from local timber with every possible luxury roughing it. Especially when it came with catering by Tara, and a hot tub overlooking the ocean and mountains fed by spring water.

A great hurrah sounded from under the trees, and the steel band moved into their liveliest musical number.

Daisy sighed out loud as Max stepped onto the jetty and flashed a grin as wide as the ocean in her direction. He looked so happy that every second of work over the past months to create a hotel from his home seemed worth it a thousand times over.

Max.

The last few hours had passed in such a blur of working with Tara and the wonderful ladies from the estate to finalise the reception meal that Tara had had to physically turn Daisy in the direction of the shower and her wedding clothes with only an hour to go.

And poor Max had barely had time to grab his suit bag before he had been carried off by speedboat to change on the yacht.

And now here they were.

The famous chocolate cake, which had become the speciality dessert of the hotel chain following the shock win of Team Treveleyn at the hotel in Cornwall, had been finished in the nick of time. It looked terrific, and most of the children had been scrubbed fairly chocolate-free. For the moment at least.

Tara came jogging along the beach towards her, her fingers holding tightly onto Freya, who had not been swimming in her silk bridesmaid dress after all but had somehow managed to lose her flowers. Tara grinned and gave her a nod—they were ready.

This was it.

Daisy plucked a red hibiscus blossom from the shrubbery next to the hotel and popped it behind Freya's ear, making her giggle with pleasure.

With one final glance to Tara, who had shared her spray of orchids with Freya, Daisy took a deep breath and stepped forward onto the sun-warmed, coral-tinged sand. The opening bars of the 'Wedding March' beaten out on steel drums drifted out seawards from behind her, but she only had eyes for one person.

The Greek-god-handsome man standing under an arch of plaited vines, hibiscus and orchids which stood on the edge of the water. Waiting to say his vows—waiting for her to agree to become his wife.

She barely noticed the friends and family, new and old, who had turned up *en masse* with smiling faces to share her happiness in the January sunshine.

This was her church. Her stained glass was the colour of the sky and the myriad shades of green from the tropical forests reflected back from the mirror-like ocean. The sweet perfume of the flowers from her headdress and bouquet filled her head with dreamy perfection at every step.

Max was wearing a white suit and white shirt, and looked so handsome as he grinned at her that it took her breath away.

Her every step across the sand, feeling the grains between her toes, was taking her closer to this remarkable man that she loved.

Of all the people in this world he had chosen *her* to spend his life with.

This man loved her.

He had given her a new home and a new family.

He was where her heart was.

In those strong arms she knew she'd found a love for the rest of her life.

It was amazing what you could achieve with a few chocolate boobs.

* * * * *

Mills & Boon® Large Print

July 2012

ROCCANTI'S MARRIAGE REVENGE
Lynne Graham

THE DEVIL AND MISS JONES
Kate Walker

SHEIKH WITHOUT A HEART
Sandra Marton

SAVAS'S WILDCAT
Anne McAllister

A BRIDE FOR THE ISLAND PRINCE
Rebecca Winters

THE NANNY AND THE BOSS'S TWINS
Barbara McMahon

ONCE A COWBOY...
Patricia Thayer

WHEN CHOCOLATE IS NOT ENOUGH...
Nina Harrington

0612 Rom LP

Mills & Boon® Large Print
August 2012

A DEAL AT THE ALTAR
Lynne Graham

RETURN OF THE MORALIS WIFE
Jacqueline Baird

GIANNI'S PRIDE
Kim Lawrence

UNDONE BY HIS TOUCH
Annie West

THE CATTLE KING'S BRIDE
Margaret Way

NEW YORK'S FINEST REBEL
Trish Wylie

THE MAN WHO SAW HER BEAUTY
Michelle Douglas

THE LAST REAL COWBOY
Donna Alward

THE LEGEND OF DE MARCO
Abby Green

STEPPING OUT OF THE SHADOWS
Robyn Donald

DESERVING OF HIS DIAMONDS?
Melanie Milburne

0712 Rom LP